THE OTHER AMERICA

Decio De Carvalho

Copyright © 2005 by Decio de Carvalho

The Other America
by Decio de Carvalho

Printed in the United States of America

ISBN 1-59781-512-8

Unless otherwise indicated, Bible quotations are taken from
the King James Version of the Bible.

www.xulonpress.com

This book is dedicated to

The Moms and Dads
Who are compelled by the love of their God,
Their country,
and their loved ones,
To laboriously homeschool their children

And

To my godly wife of 46 years
Whose people I made my people,
And whose God I made my God.

Acknowledgements

I love America. I want to show my gratitude for all she has meant to me. Yet as my reasons to be grateful and my determination to suitably express it increased through the years, so did my fears for the nation increase. This unique country I chose as home is slipping away from under God. Recently it has become clear to me that second to a true spiritual revival the steady growth of the homeschooling movement can yet prove to be a force capable of steering the nation back to the God of her fathers. With this conviction came the answer to my quest for a meaningful way to express my gratitude to America. This book is that answer.

By the time my mind and heart finished toiling with the manuscript, I found my gratefulness extended to those who helped me put the book together. First on that list is my dear wife who forgivingly cut short the "honey-do" list while I typed away in our basement. Then, I must thank Robert Williams, our caring son-in-law who half-succeeded in teaching this old dog a new trick—how to use this new-fangled thing called a computer! Most of all, I thank the two homeschooling mothers who typed the manuscript and edited it: Kathie Sickler and Bethany Hargett. I still can't understand where Bethany found the time to do the final time-consuming editing and typing, with her ten children and responsibilities as their mother and teacher, as well as pastor's wife. But that she did. You have the proof of it in your hands.

I am also very grateful to Kathie's and Bethany's home-schooled children who, like all our friends' children taught at home, inspired the writing of the novel with their unsoiled youth. Their wholesomeness furnished me with the proper colors needed to depict a main character with the virtues and knowledge I consider the active ingredients for the healing of our nation.

Thank you America. Thank you, Americans!

Decio de Carvalho
Lake Ariel, PA. May 25, 2005

Contents

Part One

Part Two

Part One

CHAPTER 1

A Twentieth Century Pilgrim

Mark Targett got ready to work through another uneventful day. He hated sameness as much as he hated his temporary job. Tuesday was usually a slow day at the electronic store. Quitting time seemed like an eternity away. Then suddenly, by mid-morning, things changed abruptly. The sameness that bored him so would not return for a long time.

Mark's boss always made sure that a number of TV sets were turned on all day in order to attract customers. An announcer's nervous voice cut through his thoughts, compelling him to notice the screen. Was this to be the beginning of another fictitious, shocking story? Not when the voice feeding the suspense in a somber tone was that of the regular morning news reporter. The newscaster sounded alarmed, tense, but not theatrical. It was evident that he was describing the scene of events occurring even then.

At that moment, a foreign-looking man burst through the door. His sudden appearance made Mark miss the reporter's actual words. The visitor's intense manner alerted Mark to keep a watch on him. Too many thefts had been occurring lately. Mark had never seen this man before.

He could not guess his nationality.

The newcomer was the only other person in the store. He strode to the nearest television set and planted himself before the appliance, his eyes fixed upon the screen. What was he looking for? Could he be trusted? These questions were eclipsed by the sight Mark's horrified eyes caught on the television. One of the World Trade Center towers had a huge multi-story rent in it from which poured billows of smoke and fire. The special report explained how an airliner had flown right into it. Incredibly, another huge airliner entered the screen, flying dangerously low. The aircraft could not maintain its altitude and direction without collision. Before he could grasp the full intent, he saw the enormous airplane plunge into the other tower. Surely, this was a nightmarish dream or a Hollywood-concocted scene of violence. The tall building swallowed the enormous jet, leaving a gaping gash. In the confusing scene of fire, rescue, terror, fear, and pitiless death, swirling emotions filled Mark's heart.

Mark was not accustomed to showing his sentiments, but astonishment and dismay dominated as he gaped at the screen. He found it difficult to accept what he was witnessing. This was no special effect gimmick construed in a film lab. Shaken, Mark imagined hundreds, possibly thousands of mangled, burning bodies inside the burning buildings.

With a sickening wrench the top of the tower above the gash of the second tower toppled and the whole structure came crashing down. The huge tower simply was no more. Hundreds of real people who had been living, breathing, and working normally just minutes before were trapped and crushed in mounds of twisted and splintered concrete and glass. Minutes later the other tower also crumbled to the ground in a cloud of dust, fire, smoke, and ash. There was only empty space where the giant skyscrapers had once stood strong and proud.

For a moment, not a sound came from the TV speakers.

The reporter seemed at a loss for words. Mark could almost hear his own heart beating. His mind was numb. This was happening in America?

A motion from beyond him reminded Mark of the other man's presence. He now observed deep lines of grief and sorrow in his face, as he was struggling in the grips of some deep and powerful emotion. Abruptly, the newcomer walked to an empty corner of the showroom. There, facing the wall, he buried his face in his hands and wept soundlessly. Only the heaving of his back and shoulders spoke of the intensity of his weeping.

Mark experienced another emotion new to him. In his many hours of TV viewing, he had lived through pain, horror, and fear only by proxy. But these people he had seen plunging from the doomed skyscrapers to be shattered on the pavement tens of floors below belonged not to stunt men. The man weeping in his store was not being paid to make others cry. Outside of films, Mark had never seen a man weep before. He found himself strangely drawn to the foreigner. As he neared him, Mark discovered that he was an old man, much older than he had previously thought.

Sensing Mark's nearness, the older man dried his eyes and turned to look at the younger man. Mark was still at a loss as to what to do or say. His sympathetic gesture must have conveyed his intention for the old man answered an unasked question. With genuine consternation in his voice, he spoke with a foreign accent: "I am sorry. I weep for my America in labor pains. I fear for her life when she has to give birth to the Other America."

After a brief, poignant meeting of their eyes, the old man briefly nodded, excused himself, and walked to the door. But now slowly, heavily.

CHAPTER 2

Investigations

On the first Sunday after the tragedy already labeled Nine-eleven, Mark woke up pensively. He had suffered from bad dreams all night. Visions of an old man weeping in a store corner had mixed with billows of flame and smoke, body parts, and collapsing buildings. He had slept restlessly and woke with an inner dissatisfaction with the way things were.

He lay there reflecting on the unfolding events of the past week. He reviewed the attack and destruction of the towers, the attempt at the Pentagon, and the double hijacking of another plane in Pennsylvania. Flitting back into his mind was a scene of his high school days.

He and Donna had been walking to McDonalds after what Mark had thought was a silly history test. They were both seniors then and had shared the same subjects and classrooms. His girlfriend glanced sideways at him and started talking about that test. She was not deterred when Mark only grunted in reply. Her words were really irritating him. Unaware of her friend's vexation, she laughed, "How did you fill in the blanks where we were to write the names of three of the most prominent founders of America?"

Mark angrily kicked an empty, dented soda can from the sidewalk and blurted, "I put down Humphrey Bogart, Hugh Heffner, and Marilyn Monroe. There!"

Donna's noisy laughter broke his peevish mood, and changed the subject of their conversation. But as they sat later, hunched over their hamburgers, he remembered reflecting that his latest history textbook had given more space for Hollywood stars than to George Washington. He knew that the same treatment was given to other "old fogies," as most kids were calling these first leaders of his country.

Again, the scenes from his tortured dreams danced before him. He would not think of these things. Hadn't he trained himself to be tough since his father had abandoned his mother and the two children? That was when he was nine. And hadn't his self-induced toughness served him well when he refused to place his hand on his chest while mumbling the Pledge of Allegiance? He had felt it was a farce, a ceremony with empty meaning. He had been called to task for his rebellion, but had stood his ground.

As he mulled over his thoughts, it seemed the foreigner stood before him. Mark had followed him outside the building on that eventful Tuesday. What had Mark intended to do? What could he have said to the man? Was there anything that could have been said? The old man's answer to the question he had never asked astounded him. The stranger's words were odd, cryptic. He realized that the foreigner's reference to America, whatever his strange words meant, was probably what had prompted him to follow the old man.

He had watched from the store entrance as the man walked to his car. He hadn't even been aware of Mark's attention, as he had eased into his red '91 Dodge Caravan. Mark had heard him start the car. He sat alone in the van staring straight ahead. Then he leaned on the steering wheel as if a new wave of grief was sweeping over him. Mark had stood silently watching, wondering why such grief, and what his statement about the labor pains of America had meant. When the older man had apparently calmed down, he backed out of his parking spot toward the storefront, giving Mark a good view of the vehicle's registration. It had been a Pennsylvania plate. The number was one Mark would not easily forget—DKF 7110.

With a long luxurious stretch, Mark abruptly cut his thoughts short and set to think about his plans for the day. This was the one Sunday of the month he was off work all day. Some businessmen still paid a token to the blue laws by not opening their places of business until one o' clock. "Just to accommodate church-going people," muttered Mark, to himself, irritably.

Going to church was the last thing he ever wanted to do. He hoped to spend this day reading. He still had not read the book written by Al Gore that his activist friends who were concerned with pollution were talking about. Donna had given him a hardcover copy of the book on his birthday before she left for Florida. But after flicking on the news, and being plunged into conjecture and discussion on the tragedy again, he changed his mind. They were still counting bodies. The public was told that some of them would never be recovered. They figured the death toll could reach the thousands. While sympathizing with the families of the victims, Mark brought the old man at the store vividly to his mind again. Every detail of the unforgettable scene came back to him this chilly Sunday morning, including the old man's car registration number. Mark turned off the television and picked up the phone.

Joe Colletti, his mother's boy friend, was a policeman just promoted to the investigation department. His home and office numbers were listed on a telephone pad. Mark wondered whether Joe was on duty. It wouldn't hurt to try. He punched the officer's work number first. Yes, Mr.

Colletti was there, but he was busy. Mark left a message. Ten minutes later Mark's telephone rang.

"What's up, buddy?"

Mark recognized the imperious voice of Officer Colletti. Their relationship with each other was cordial, but hardly considered friendly. The older man always tried to please his friend's son, but he rarely succeeded.

"I need a favor from you. I don't know how busy you are with all that's been happening lately, but is it too much of a hassle to find the name and address of someone by his car registration number?"

The investigator knew that he could meet such a request in minutes. But he hesitated. He was trained to ask the circumstances that raised the need. Should he ask Mark why he needed the information? What was his purpose in wanting it? But his desire to please won out at the end.

"No hassle at all. Are you in some kind a trouble?" he asked patronizingly.

"Heavens, no! Just someone I met at the store, an old, mild gentleman whom I'd like to know better."

"And all you have is the man's car registration number, correct?" Mr. Colletti could not help being an investigator. He was wondering how much effort had been applied by Mark to secure that number. But he waved aside all caution. "What is the number? Pennsylvania registration, you say?"

Mark told him.

One hour later, his telephone rang. Joe Colletti had the name, address and telephone number of the owner of a '91 Dodge Caravan registration number DKF 7110. He had found quite a bit of personal data on "the subject," as his profession calls the individuals they investigate. He had made sure to find out as much as he could about a Marco Nemo, male, 103 Church Rd., Canaan, PA. But the name and address were all he let Mark know. Even Mr. Nemo's telephone number was not included in the information he passed on to the inquirer. He wanted Mark to find that for himself if he needed it.

Now that he had the old man's name and address, Mark wondered about his real purpose for getting it. Did he want to contact him? He would have to make up his mind. Should he write him? Call him? Drive by? He felt he had to justify doing any one of the three. What was he after anyway? "I can act on this information whenever I like," He finally decided.

He read the first chapters of Gore's book for a while, but caught himself flipping pages as his eyes swept through without any concentration. He caught himself musing over recollections of when his grandfather was still living. He had been a gentle, fatherly man and Mark had loved him dearly. He died when Mark was only six. Grandfather and grandson compressed much love and show of affection within that short period of time. There was something warm about his Papa, as Mark called him. Grandfather was always kind to him. Often while on long rides in his black Oldsmobile, he would talk with Mark as if he were a grown-up. Mark had been named after him. The memories of two old men, Marco and Mark, kept intervening between the points the former Vice-President was trying to make in his book and Mark's ability to fully grasp them.

The only thing Mark didn't like about those conversations with his Papa as he remembered them was that he was always talking about God. Mark had not felt this way at the time, but came to realize it when he was in high school. That was when he began to dislike Christians. But somehow, his distaste did not cool the warm memories or diminish the respect Mark had for Papa.

While eating his brunch he was still undecided on what he would do. Should he look up Marco Nemo's phone number? Maybe not. Should he drive by and see what would happen? That seemed like a good plan, since it was only fifteen miles to the burg of Canaan. He put on his winter jacket and left.

It was a chilly, foggy day, but Mark's well-kept Honda started promptly as always. He had bought it second-hand when he was seventeen and worked after school at the electronic store. The dashboard clock informed him that it was a quarter-to-one. He knew where Church Road was. He could be there in twenty minutes. What should he say if he saw him? He was still not too sure of what he was doing. What if Mr. Marco Nemo's emotional breakdown was the result of mental instability? And if he were a mentally stable man, would he feel bad meeting someone who had witnessed his weakness? Had it even been a demonstration of weakness or was it the result of a soft, compassionate heart? And why should he care what caused a man to break down emotionally and weep convulsively? Was the old man just "weeping over his beer" as he had heard someone express recently? No! Somehow, Mark felt that it was for this nation's pains that he had wept. "For my America," he had said. The emphasis was striking. Nearing his destination, Mark slowed down and turned onto Church Road.

The number 103 was written boldly on a white stone neatly placed at the entrance gate of an old house. Its recently installed vinyl siding covered well the old boards but did nothing to conceal its age. The style and size spoke of an old farm homestead well over one hundred years old. It reminded him of the farmhouse in which he had grown up in upstate New York. He looked at the mysterious Mr. Nemo's place with a mixture of homesickness and sadness. He stayed parked across from the farmhouse, trying to decide whether he really wanted to make acquaintance with its dweller or not. There was no indication of anybody being home. Mark was still hesitating when he realized that if his car was seen there with the engine running and he inside he would have no choice but to announce his intention of visiting. Thinking this, he accelerated the Honda and drove slowly northwards. Just then, he saw the red Dodge Caravan pass him, going south and noted that the brake lights came on right before the old house. Mark drove a little further, found a hidden driveway in some woods, and used it to turn around. He hoped the couple he had seen in the red van had not witnessed this maneuver. On his return, he saw the old man in the house's driveway opening the passenger door for an elderly woman. His wife?

Mark didn't bother to answer his own question. He noticed something about Marco Nemo that quickly changed the "Shall-I-Shall-I-Not" game. The old man carried a thick black Bible under his arm. The couple was just coming back from church, evidently one of those churches frequented by far right conservatives determined still to believe in make-believe. Mark amusedly recalled how he had watched former President Clinton on television three or four years earlier coming out of a church with a black Bible under his arm, just like this Nemo person. That had been on a Sunday morning also. Mark remembered being initially upset about it, but then he realized that his leader was a real political genius. He knew what he was doing. Besides, for years the man had been giving ample proofs of not being one of those silly Bible-thumping Christians who believed America to be a Christian nation. He had a right to be as good an actor as Mr. Reagan. At the end, Mark had laughed about the incident. But somehow, he could not allow himself to laugh about Marco Nemo and his big black Bible. And he didn't know why. This new unanswered question was added to the many other questions dancing in his brain since Nine-eleven. Meanwhile, he would go back to Al Gore and his yet unfulfilled dream of saving the nation's environment. He must forget all about Marco Nemo.

Mark revved his CRX engine and headed home. The thought that Donna being there would have given him a

needed diversion from his overworked brain simply tanta-
lized him. He could have used a break from the flood of
questions demanding answers.

CHAPTER 3

Roots of Agnosticism

Mark Targett was proud of his skepticism. He thought that skepticism, like humor, denoted intelligence. By the time he had entered the elementary school he had started doubting everything and everyone. The roots of his agnosticism had started to grow much earlier in his childhood, well watered by his recent life experience with abandonment and Papa's death. His first teachers in kindergarten who had cleverly laced the children's games with what their mentors called "behavior modification" and "situation ethics" theories sowed the seeds. Many well-meaning schoolteachers had welcomed those ideas as signs of a healthy evolutionary thinking and had hastened to adapt them to their methodology. Healthy children's minds are naturally fertile ground. This is especially true when the student is a bright child. Little Mark's mind had been sharpened well by early suffering. There the roots of doubt grew deep and strong. Later, elementary school textbooks questioning the nation's history, morals, and traditional social mores helped to form the cast where his mind was to be forged.

By the time he was in high school, he had developed an unpleasant love-hate relationship with words. "Words," he wrote in one of his school essays, "are a culture's ineffective device loosely agreed upon to represent things. They are impostors—they pretend to be the substance of things when they are but their stammering heralds. I cannot truthfully state that 'this is a pen' to identify the object I am writing with, for I cannot say 'a pen is this' because to millions of people what I am writing with is a 'plume'. Both words have been playing their heralding game with people by pretending to be feathers."

When his English teacher first read that play on words, he was impressed. But when he saw Mark in his next class, he called the writer to his desk. "When you copy something," he told Mark, "you must use quotation marks to separate what you wrote from somebody else's writing. And you must always give credit to the author you are quoting from."

The teacher had spoken this loudly; the rest of the class heard him. At first, Mark was aghast at the teacher's faux pas and got ready to defend himself. But before he opened his mouth, he recognized the instructor as a fellow skeptic.

"OK," Mark answered the teacher with that condescending smile that he became so well known for as he matured into a young adult.

Later on, the English teacher acknowledged to himself that he had made a mistake, which he could have simply avoided by giving credit to the quality of the rest of the essay. But skeptic people are often blinded by their superciliousness. The weed of jealousy grows easily on the minds of skeptics. He could well have been jealous, instead of proud, of his precocious student. Could that have been the reason for his blunder?

Mark didn't mind the red B he saw written on the paper when he was expecting an A. As he walked back to his desk with a wry smile on his face, he mused: "If words are flagrant liars, what should you expect their letters to be but little brats? What can keep me from taking this guy's *B* to mean *Bravo*! And myself giving him a *D* for his situation ethics behavior? *D* for *dunce*," he added to himself, hardly able to control his laughter. He had not realized yet what he was to learn later, that cynicism seems often to follow in the wake of skepticism. At that time, he still thought of himself as just a funny person, not a cynic.

When Mark entered college backed by a scholarship and reinforced financially by part-time work, that character flaw showed up soon enough. The term "got out of the closet" was how he would have described it then, had he realized it was happening. The choice of the phrase glibly going around the campus at the time would have indicated his interest and involvement in the many human rights movements he found on the college campus.

From the beginning of his college days Mark's agnostic, politically activist professors received him as a human trophy. They had little to add to his beliefs and no need to teach him unbelief as they felt themselves duty bound to do to their students. His political science professor, a young, ambitious Harvard graduate, quickly identified his new student as a gifted young man. He didn't take long in electing himself Mark's personal tutor. But, to his disappointment, the position was not to keep him too busy in the coming days.

"You'll go a long ways, Mark!" he told his favorite student when first reading one of Mark's essays. But the affected way with which he said it disturbed Mark. It seemed to him that the professor's body language was ad-libbing on what came out of his mouth. What he felt the professor was saying was, "You'll go a long way—with me." Since that day and throughout the school year Mark saw ways to communicate to Professor Knutsen in his own body language that he wanted to keep their teacher-student relationship just that. The professor had the right to be the human being he wanted to be; let Nature choose who he was to be. Human rights, he concluded to himself, started at home. When he found out a few years later that Dr. Knutsen had joined Senator John Kerry's staff as his advisor on gay rights, he would remember that statement.

By the end of his first year Mark had become the most sought after contributor to the student paper. And he was unanimously elected editor of the *Listen Up!* for the coming year when Nelly Kelly, the present editor, was to leave for Princeton. Nelly Kelly was her real name, not a clever pen name. Many considered her the most progressive activist on campus. This adjective was designed to make attractive the umbrella under which her paper spelled out the students' socio-political beliefs. When Mark met her, after they had discussed his first contribution to the weekly paper, he asked her what she was going to take up at Princeton. Her answer would drive him to do some further reading on the progressive ideology the paper espoused. "I want to be a church minister," she had replied.

As for Mark, it had become axiomatic that journalism was to be his career. He welcomed the opportunity to start his training. He was looking forward to joining the army of pundits in the media crusading for a better world and, as he perceived, a less conceited America. He would do his best to stop words from playing games, especially religious ones, and he would make them become, instead, soldiers properly armed with the weapons of change. That was when he had dropped Cummings, his father's name, and became just Mark Targett, like his dear Papa.

Like many of his educated peers, he believed his nation to be an obnoxious hurdle in the way of societal evolution. He felt that America was holding back human progress by hoarding more than her share of worldly goods and defending her greed with a sword in one hand and a Bible in the other. Nelly Kelly must know something about religion that he didn't yet know. He would have to learn what it was so he could decide whether to join her or help destroy the myth once and for all. Mark Targett was his own man even though he wanted to participate in the oneness of the secular brotherhood his education was teaching him. Life and future loomed as a challenge before him. And he was ready for it.

CHAPTER 4

Christmas Emptiness

By the end of the Nine-eleven year, the cultural war truce was still holding. But both sides knew well that that wouldn't last. The lowering of the white flag would be hardly noticed in the midst of the profusion of red, white, and blue banners proclaiming everywhere the nation's re-awakened patriotism. But no armistice leading to lasting peace had been negotiated. By the beginning of the following year, verbal shots, only temporarily deadened by cautious silencers, were heard. They were coming from anti-America die-hards in the media and from the lecterns of academia. The silencers were meant to prove that the protesters were patriots too. But they had already made America and the world know that theirs was a flagless patriotism; that they had a more enlightened understanding of that virtue.

Since Mark was only a few months short of completing his journalism degree, in December he took time away from work to visit his university in Philadelphia. He must arrange to run his last academic stretch. He would miss the campus activities that he had participated in during the short time that he had been a resident student.

In one of the student lounges, he picked up a copy of the *Free Student*, the campus newspaper. Mark had been the editor of that paper also for the year he lived there. The subject of terrorism was still the theme of the weekly paper. And so was patriotism—the flagless type. There was not much in the publication about the political activities so common before Nine-eleven, but the Anti-War Coalition, one of the students' organizations, had scheduled a meeting for Sunday. Professor Shorham, Dean of Social Studies at Yale, was to be the main speaker. Mark noticed a few other advertisements for lectures on the various schools of eastern mysticism. Holistic medicine practitioners were still busy seeking adherents. Meditation workshops under Guru Mandra Savandra were programmed for right after the spring break. It seemed that Professor Shorham was going to have a large audience. He had little competition for the weekend. The few other traditional religious activities were unpopular and scarce.

Mark stayed with friends, fellow students who lived outside the university city. They told him about the various parties being held on campus that weekend. But Mark was not much for partying. He would spend his days in Philadelphia making arrangements for housing for when he returned to secure the credits he still needed to complete his course. On Sunday, he would be at the Eisenhower Hall. He was not going to miss Dr. Shorham's lecture. Mark had read his books and articles. They were plentifully available in the university's library.

Mark had a difficult time getting back to Honesdale on Tuesday. Five inches of snow had blanketed northeastern Pennsylvania. The temperature had hovered in the teens. Sleet had followed the snow as frigid winds blew from the Canadian northland. Mark had promised Bob Shaffer, the electronic storeowner, that he would be back at work on

Wednesday. Mr. Shaffer had been good to him. He had provided Mark with a job and a work schedule to accommodate the time of his classes since his high school days. Mark had his defects, but ingratitude and lack of commitment were not among them. Though tempted to stay with his friends in Philadelphia and wait for a break in the cold spell, Mark decided to brave the weather. He was going to trust his little front wheel drive car to get him back home.

The Pennsylvania Turnpike was still open, though the traffic was the least Mark had ever seen. The road maintenance crew had done a good job in keeping the highway passable. It took him almost four hours to reach Honesdale instead of the normal two-and-a-half. He wouldn't have to break his promise to his boss, even though there would be few customers at the store.

Three winters before, the Santillis had rented the little upstairs apartment in their Honesdale home to Mark. The landlord had retired from the New York City Fire Department. The elderly couple could visit with their children in New York and New Jersey as often as they wanted and then could spend the whole winter in Florida where they owned a trailer permanently installed in a trailer park in Kissimmee. Mark minded the house while they were away. In return for this arrangement, Mark was able to have a place to live for low rent.

Mark arrived back to an empty house. Like winter-weary birds, the Santillis had already flown south. They had left earlier then they had anticipated. The note he found stuck to the refrigerator read that, though having planned to leave after Christmas, they wanted to beat the threatening snowstorm. The note, obviously written by Mrs. Santilli, ended with "*Have a happy Holiday*" and "*Love ya,*" a colloquialism they learned in the south.

Mark realized that having a house all to himself had its drawbacks. He was lonely. Mark had seen houses and businesses being gradually adorned with myriad of lights and Christmas symbols all throughout the months of November and December. He had the same love-hate relationship with Christmas that he had with words. Mark had not realized until he got home that it was Christmas Day.

After three active days in Philadelphia with people around all the time, his little bachelor apartment made Mark feel disconnected from the world. He sat on his couch, tired. His only guest was that bittersweet feeling of loneliness to numb him. He remembered the radio and television in front of him, ensconced inside the amusement center. He had bought the furniture at the local Salvation Army for next to nothing. Those inventions were designed to bring the world to the viewer, so Mark turned the TV on. He quickly identified the seasonal, Christmassy "Miracle on Fifth Avenue" fantasy being played. He grimaced. "That's all I need now," he mumbled to himself. He didn't bother changing channels. He turned the TV off and the radio on. The voice he heard thundering out of the speakers was fraught with self-confidence and optimism: "WITH TALENTS ON LOAN FROM GOD!" The word *God* sounded as if there were five "*o*'s" between the consonants, every one of them sounding like awe.

"Limbaugh! Even on Christmas Day! Warmed-over fare, obviously." Mark spewed the show host's name with contempt and turned the radio off abruptly. He was not only lonely, he was angry. That short phrase had triggered a memory of the same man saying that soldiers were supposed to kill people and destroy things. Mark muttered darkly to himself, "That's what millions of people are learning from that media mogul."

Those stabbing words brought to his mind Professor Shorham's lecture. The speaker had quoted those very same ugly words when decrying the late heavy attack on Afghanistan by our overwhelming military forces. What he had said after that had visibly moved his activist hearers. Mark tried to remember his exact words. They came to him almost verbatim: "Picture the Middle East and the Arab world as a giant powder keg floating on a sea of oil. This warmongering administration has just lit the fuse leading to it. When the American-made match's flame reaches the detonator the conflagration will be larger than ten thousand Nine-elevens!" And after those pontificating words came the reluctant, comico-gloomy pun, seriously delivered and, probably ad-libbed: "May Mr. Bush's God deliver us!"

Professor Shorham's audience had laughed, though feebly and apologetically, when they heard the derisive quip. Perhaps they were imagining millions of bodies burning in a sea of Middle East oil in flames.

Mark snorted, "Why can't America follow this peace-loving man and others like him in the way of international concord and harmony so clearly marked? Bush's God! Who is He? If He is not keeping Bush from lighting the fuse why should I care for the two of them?"

A poem by Longfellow that he had memorized years back came to his mind. Mark recited it to himself quietly, pensively, in the cadence of the bells that might have inspired the poet:

> I heard the bells on Christmas Day
> Their old, familiar chorus play,
> And wild and sweet the words repeat
> Of peace on earth, good-will to men.
>
> I thought how, as the day had come,
> The belfries of all Christendom
> Had rolled along the unbroken song
> Of peace on earth, good-will to men.

And in despair I bowed my head;
"There is no peace on earth!", I said,
For hate is strong and mocks the song
Of peace on earth, good-will to men.

There could be more verses, but Mark no longer remembered them. By the time he recited what he could still recall,
an immense sadness besieged him and overpowered his
anger. Loneliness had descended on him more fiercely than
before and this time he could not fight it off.

In the dark aloneness, Mark wept.

As he recovered from his frayed emotions, he reflected
on his three worlds. Mark had three worlds in which to feel
lonely. In the quietness of his bachelor apartment this
Christmas, he calmly enumerated them to himself. The first
was his Ideological World. Mark had lived in this world
since his high school days. That was the only world in
which he could find meaning for human life and a measure
of meaning for his own life. He credited his education for
his timely admission into this world.

Mark lived also in what he called an Illusory World
where he rubbed shoulders with only a few. In this world, he
traded words of dubious meanings with poets and musicians.
He read their poems and listened to their music. Here he also
kept company with artists who painted what they could see
to depict the unseen. The shapes and colors they engendered
were also words from a vocabulary hidden within with
meanings seldom agreed upon. In this world, Mark came
across people that he would rather avoid. Make-believing
people like the Bushes and the Nemos. Mark figured that
they bought their visas into this world with the currency of
self-delusion and they refused to acknowledge that the world
in which they were conceived was real. Those wretched men
who fly airliners into buildings lived in this illusory world
also. And so did those who fashion themselves into human

bombs to do away with others. They sacrifice what was real in order to turn illusions into reality. Mark feared what he might do if he ever fell for this world's naive enticement to fulfillment. He would then have to make himself immune to mysteries. He would have to volunteer himself for the needed abandonment of his other two worlds.

He found his third world the most difficult one to live in. It was the Real World; the world you can see in your bathroom mirror and on the streets. This was the world, which constantly maintained a series of demands more numerous than one could meet. The demands are limitless, absolute; the means to meet the demands rationed, restricted.

Mark knew that he could never be happy until all his three worlds became one. Mustn't things have three dimensions before one can know they are there? The tools of education do a good job of teaching about concrete things, but they are utterly inadequate in dealing reliably with the abstract.

For the first time in his twenty-three years of life, Mark started to suspect that something vital to human life had been extracted from him at the dawning of his reasoning. He found himself unable to tell what it could have been, where it was disposed of, and whether it could be retrieved. He couldn't tell either, why he could visualize Marco Nemo weeping for his America.

The sight was mingling with the winter scene outside his window. But he knew that it was not because of the whiteness of the man's hair, nor the winter of life it speaks of. "Words, words..." he murmured to himself. " Will they ever tell me who they are instead of what they fraudulently represent?—I must be cracking up under the spell of winter magic—Christmas magic!"

Mark rebelled against that train of thought. He would find something to eat. His eyes fell on his mail neatly piled on top of the refrigerator by one of the Santillis. He had forgotten to inspect it when coming in. He picked up the envelopes and returned to the couch. Mark identified two of the envelopes as containing bills. In another, he knew he would find the never tiring coaxing for him to sign up for credit cards at zero percent interest. He bypassed those. He immediately recognized the senders of two of the three remaining envelopes. One was from his sister in Oregon, and one from his mother who lived in the village of Galilee a few miles away. As for the third letter, he had to peer at it intently before the tightly lettered address brought a smile of recognition. But his smile was not out of contentment. He rarely heard from his father and it didn't fit his mood. That one could wait.

He decided to open his sister's letter first. It was a Kwanzaa card. "What in the world!" Mark thought in surprise. He read it. After the sugary wishes, there was a note in Mendy's rough handwriting. With few, direct words she informed her younger brother that she had finally discovered her call in life. She had joined a gay rights movement and found herself active and happy with what she was doing. She was happy also with the steadiness of her latest relationship. Sandy was a very nice girl, she told her brother. Mark smiled again, but again, not out of contentment. Her confession was no surprise to him.

His big surprise came inside his mother's envelope. Not only because this was the first time he had received mail from her since he had left home, but also because it was a Christmas card. An innocent looking one, with Magi, angels, a manger with a blond baby in it, and the robed couple surrounded by the usual menagerie. Mark was familiar with his mother's tastes. He knew she didn't mind this Christmas thing, but then, she had never had her heart in it. She was not the kind to take delight in its icons. "What gives?" he asked. The answer was on the blank side of the card, written in his mother's neat handwriting. There was purposefulness in her careful writing: "Dear Son, what I have to tell you is so important to me that I had to write instead of call. Besides, I had to see this in writing myself. Mark, I have just become a Christian. I feel like a new person since I made that decision. I am sure you will love your new mother. I hope to be able to tell you all about it soon. Have a blessed Christmas! Love, Mother."

This news stunned Mark. "And now this!" he cried. He threw the card on his coffee table, rested his elbows on his knees, and covered his face with his hands. He had never felt so much at a loss as to what to think or feel since his grandfather had died, and then, when his best friend had died. He sensed a rift in his armor of protection against unwanted emotions. Could he correct it?

His loneliness returned, this time with a mind to stay. Mark forgot that he had been feeling hungry when he had come into the empty house. He felt hurt, deeply hurt. Mark wished to die. Die? Did he really wish to die on a Christmas Day? Death. He remembered how much more meaning he had found in the word when Bobby had died. His best friend had just turned fifteen when Bobby's father had found the note on the dashboard of his old Ford Mercury parked in the outside garage. The engine had been hot and was still running. The heavy garage door had been locked. Mr. Webster had struggled to open it without the garage door opener. He had just seen and smelled the bluish exhaust fumes pouring innocently from under it. The youth's body was slumped on the front seat. The curtness in the choice of words of his last communication with his small, unhappy world was just like Bobby. He had scrawled carelessly on his school note pad folded in half: "Good-bye, world. I don't think it is worth being around any more."

It had been Christmas Day when his best friend had killed himself. Thousands of teenagers had done the same thing since then. But, then why did they do it? As if waking up from a bad dream, Mark picked up his mother's card again. He noticed, for the first time, printed prettily under the manger's scene: "*PEACE ON EARTH, GOOD WILL TO MEN!*" He walked to the stove still holding the card and lit up one gas burner. He held the card above the blue flame and watched it burn. While the card burned, Mark muttered, "Burn, burn, pretty Mama's card with pretty, lying words! Take my place in death until I am ready to follow you. I still have a job to do!" The burning smell filled the air in his efficiency kitchen. Leaving the rest of the card to burn by itself, he picked up the phone and pressed a few keys. The eleven beeps disclosed that he had punched a long distance number. A few seconds went by.

Miles away someone responded.

"Hi, Donna! This is Mark. Donna..." he paused, waiting for a deep breath to run its course in his chest, "I love you!"

Mark had never said that to anybody.

CHAPTER 5

Enter—a Light!

❦

At eight o'clock Wednesday morning, Mark was at his post at Shaffer's store. Despite the weather, the mall was already getting crowded. The yearly ritual of returning and exchanging merchandise had started. Like New Yorkers, Pennsylvanians are used to taking snow and ice in stride. Bob Shaffer was already there at the helm of his profitable business.

"How did it go in Philly, Mark?" He wanted to know. And he really did.

"Fine, Mr. Shaffer. I shall be leaving you for good at springtime break. I might need some time off in between, if I could. They want me to have a few more credits in political science before I can tackle the remaining classes."

"Remind me one week before you have to leave me again, Mark. I'll work with you. So we'll be loosing you for good by spring, then. We'll miss you. You are a good man, Charley Brown," he quipped. Bob Shaffer was a Peanuts cartoon aficionado. "Will that job in Scranton that Joe Colletti was arranging for you really pan out?"

"It looks that way, Mr. Shaffer. I had a good interview with the chief editor. Crime reporting is not what I intend to spend my life doing. But it is a start. The newspaper has a solid position in the community. They seem confident I can fit in."

Businessmen are skillful in the use of their time where it best counts for profitability. Bob Shaffer was no exception. The conversation ended abruptly. That brought to Mark's mind the conversation he had with Donna the night before. It had been cut short. It made Mark uneasy. It wasn't that he feared rejection, though Donna's terseness could be an indication of that. His uneasiness was with himself. Loneliness, bad memories, and unwanted news had tricked him. They had made him lower his carefully built guard against the darts of emotionalism. He had allowed a chink in his armor. He wasn't sure what his feelings were toward the girl. He wasn't even sure whether he would ever be able to define the word love. "They say that love is blind and that seems so," he thought to himself. "Though ignorant as I am on the subject, I suspect that love is more than that. Love is a patch of ice on a slippery slope. I let myself slip and fall while in full use of my twenty/twenty vision. No wonder they say that people fall in love." He was tempted to laugh at his pun, but he resisted the temptation easily. He was too upset with himself to entertain humor.

Mark was still punishing himself mentally when his first customer entered the store. She was a young petite girl with long black hair and a smile that seemed to be a permanent feature of her face. And she was wearing a dress. Mark couldn't remember the last time he had seen a girl in a dress. She didn't wait to hear from Mark the familiar "May I help you?"

"Hi!" she said, brightly. "There's something wrong with this cell phone I bought for my grandpa in your store last week. Can you..." Mark took the phone from the girl's small hands.

"What seems to be the problem, young lady?"

"The problem doesn't seem. It is a 'fait accompli'. Just look at this battery compartment cover. It is as loose as a five-year-old's front tooth." While saying this, a smile which was almost laughter gave proof that she had no animosity.

Mark was amused. "Where does this charming creature come from?" he wondered mutely. "She's not the kind of kid we meet every day. I wonder where she learned French. It came out so easily, as if she could think in that language also. Charm plus education—a fatal combination. Watch that chink closely, Mark, boy!" Warning himself inwardly, he smiled and verified the fact of the girl's 'fait'. The little plastic cover was indeed slack.

"You are right, Miss. Looks like some Chinaman goofed on this one. No problem. We'll give you another telephone. Do you have the receipt with you?"

She did. Mark disappeared into the back storeroom. Minutes later, he returned with a new telephone. He pressed his thumb to it and tried to wiggle the plastic battery cover to be sure. It was tight.

"There," he said. "That's better. May I have your receipt, please?" The computer hummed, rang, and produced another receipt.

"Would the young lady please sign here so we can 'accompli' the correction? And where did the young lady learn French?"

"Yes, Sir!" she answered. And while signing her name—*Abigail Swingle*—"Oh, French? Sorry, it came out without my thinking. My grandpa is a polyglot and my best teacher." Mark placed the new phone back in the box, picked up the signed receipt and looked at the unpretentious signature. "A strange name for a strange girl," he thought.

"Abigail. A pretty name. I never heard the name before," he remarked, "You..."

"It is in the Bible. First Kings."

To this, Mark responded with a serious "Oh!"

Abigail was quick to notice Mark's veiled disapproval of her name's origin. But that didn't keep her from continuing to explain her name, just as if she had never detected Mark's cold reaction.

"Abigail was the widow of a very bad man. But she herself was a godly woman and King David married her for her goodness. The Bible tells us she was very pretty too."

"Just like her twenty-first century namesake!" Mark said, recovering his amiable poise. He didn't think the girl was particularly pretty. But a better kind of beauty emanated from her honest femininity. This, plus Abigail's personality and demeanor, justified Mark's assessment of the girl. "Is Abby short for Abigail?" he wanted to know.

"Bingo!" Abby answered, laughing again. "I can see you are not only a gentleman, you are a sharp young man, though not sharp enough to distinguish between a Cinderella and a Plain Jane. Thanks a million, Mr.—"

"Mark," he informed her, with a touch of humility he didn't know he had. "I thank you too."

When Abigail left the store, it seemed to Mark that the light went out of the room with her. But one of the three worlds he lived in had suddenly become darker and more oppressive than before.

CHAPTER 6

Helen

Mark's mother worked in Bethany, at the Pocono Nursing Home as its Activities Director. When she first got the job, Mark attributed it to his mother's ability to tell people what she knew they wanted to hear. He could be right. You can make good progress in any work dealing with people if you say yes more than no. Helen Cummings was good at this game. After years of practice, she could play the part without having to think. Few people realized that she really didn't care much about them and that her unconscious agreeableness was a device she had developed in order to make life easier for herself. She did not consider pretence to be a vice in diplomacy or in public relations.

The trouble was that Mark's father had seen through her. Explosive arguments and silent wars ended their marriage. Neither had she fooled Mark. He had regarded her with apathy since childhood. These events had helped to condition the soil of his heart for the seeds of skepticism his education was to sow later.

Helen loved her job and was good at keeping her senior citizens occupied. She worked long hours but did not have a work schedule. She was always at the home during uncommon events. Mark rarely saw her. He didn't mind that. Since her card at Christmas, he felt safer in shunning her the same way he was avoiding Marco Nemo.

She had called often since then, when Mark was not home. The first time, she had left a message on his answering machine. There was a note of tenderness in her voice when she ended the recording with a "Love you, Mark", but it failed to move him. He had a long history of not responding to his mother's entreaties. He didn't return the call. By the unusual number of calls the answering device had counted Mark knew that she had called more times without leaving a message.

He was in his apartment after leaving work one evening when his telephone rang. It was a Saturday evening. He suspected it was his mother calling, but, then, it could be Donna. He hadn't heard from his girlfriend since he told her something he didn't believe himself. He had said those three words through the chink he had foolishly allowed to form in his armor. Mark was curious to know what was to happen to their relationship. And the ball was in Donna's court. He answered the phone at the fourth ring, just before his recorded answer was to play its message. It was his mother.

"Hi, son!"

Mark had never attached any meaning to her motherly preference of calling him son; neither had she before intended any. He would rather be on a first name basis. The last two generations of youngsters had been encouraged to call their progenitors by their given name. Yet out of respect for Papa, he would never be able to call his grandmother Grace. And he had long ago chosen not to call his mother Helen. He made the decision, not out of respect, but because he simply knew that his mother would have been delighted with the idea. He had no inclination to please her.

"Hi, Mother," Mark answered coldly. "What's up?" Without waiting for her reply, he guessed at why she had called. "Yes, Mother, I got your Christmas card. Is that the only reason why you are calling?"

Helen didn't respond immediately. Mark never realized how his coldness was hurting her. She needed those few seconds to steady her emotions before answering. He didn't try to guess the reason for the hiatus. He would rather not know. He noticed that his mother cleared her throat before telling him the true reason for her call.

"Mark," she said quietly, "It is Granny. She is not well, Mark. The doctor wants her in the hospital for observation. He says it's just for a few days. I have been staying at the Home for the last three days..."

"Mother," Mark cut in," what will she be tested for? Does he sound concerned?" Mark himself was concerned. He had enough love for Papa to spill over to his pert wife of thirty-five years. She had always been a wiry, healthy woman. And she had high regards for her favorite grandchild who carried his Papa's name.

"He didn't seem to want to give me any detail, and that worries me. He says that only after the tests will he be able to tell what her problem is. He wants to start the tests no later than Monday morning. The problem, Mark, is that my car has been in the shop for the last four days. That's why I've been staying in the Home. I have been wondering whether you'll be off work Monday to take us to the Honesdale hospital. Dr. Schultz has already made the necessary arrangements..."

"My car is a two-seater, Mother. We might have to use a taxi," Mark interrupted Helen again. "Unless we can make two trips."

"I am sorry if I am not giving you enough time to plan this. I've been trying to reach you since Wednesday. Am I right to conclude that you'll be off on Monday and that you'll be able to help your two old ladies?"

Mark felt guilty. He remembered when he was six years old and Granny Targett had told him with many tears that

Papa was dead. He had the feeling of having betrayed Papa. He knew all along that his mother had been trying to reach him. He should have called her back.

"I am sorry I didn't call you back, Mother. Yes, I am off Monday and I'll be able to take you and Granny to the hospital. What time do we have to be there?"

"At 8:30 in the morning." Helen sounded relieved. "Is that too early for you, son?" The word *son* sounded more sincere.

"That will be OK. I'll have to be at your place at the latest by 7:30. Remember, I'll need to make two trips. You and Granny ought to strategize this. Please, call me again tomorrow and let me know which of you 'old ladies' I should pick up first. I'll be here all day, reading." Mark had said *old ladies* in a kind tone of voice, jokingly. He felt he needed to be kind and try to expiate his guilt.

After the call, Mark sat on his small sofa and let his mind wander. He thought of Nemo Marco and Papa; they seemed always intertwined in his thoughts lately. He wondered why his mother sounded more humble, less insincere. Granny Targett, he feared, wouldn't be with them much longer. He visited Donna in his thoughts, and lingered there, puzzled, questioning. Then, to his surprise, he thought of Abigail. His thoughts dwelt for a while with the spirited girl with the Biblical name. Mark didn't know much about her, for sure, but he liked what he learned by her simple presence and behavior. She had her own Papa whom she seemed to love enough to buy an expensive phone. Did Abby ever treat him as he did his mother and Granny Targett?

Mark tried to examine objectively the recent chink in his armor. It seemed a little wider since the telephone had rung fifteen minutes ago. He shook his head and shepherded his thoughts back to himself, to his real world. Danger lay in leaving thoughts too long in the path that leads to illusion.

The real Mark was hungry. He had not had a bite to eat

since noon. Part of his present reality was that there was nothing much in the refrigerator. He would go to the Honesdale Diner for a late dinner, then to the supermarket for groceries. They stayed open all night. He would stay in the apartment all day the next day, and needed some provisions. Mark put his winter coat on and walked out into the street.

CHAPTER 7

A Hospital Visit

Early next Monday Mark drove to Galilee to pick up his mother. Helen was ready and waiting. As they had planned the day before, they went first to Grandmother's place. Grace Targett was not ready, but still they were able to leave in time to make the two short trips to the hospital. He took Grandmother first and left her seated cozily in the hospital waiting room while he went back to fetch his mother. They didn't talk much on the way and that was not like mother. "She sure doesn't act like her old, domineering self," he mused.

At the hospital parking lot, when Mark noticed her struggling to get out of his diminutive two-seater he walked around the car and helped her out. He took her hand and she smiled demurely. He expected her to come up with some sweet pleasantry about Mark's courtesy. But as she stood to her feet, she just whispered feelingly, "Thanks, Mark." While walking toward the reception room Mark wondered about the woman walking quietly beside him holding on to his arm. He concluded that his mother was getting old. She seemed to be weary of her life of deception.

Mark took his grandmother's place as Mother led her to

the hospital's reception desk. There were papers to fill out before the elderly lady was settled. Others were in the room waiting for someone or for something to happen, their faces expressionless, lost in the anonymity of public rooms, but Mark hardly noticed them. He looked over the choice of reading materials. The *News Week* and other magazine material was all about Afghanistan, the suicide bombings in Israeli cities and threats of invasion of Iraq. Mark just scanned the pages, saw the pictures of tragedy and blood in full color, and felt depressed. He put the magazine aside. A heavy-set woman next to him stood up. She placed the book she was reading on the seat she vacated. It was a Bible. "Very fitting," Mark thought sarcastically. She must be a misfit, and needed this crutch. The uncharitable thought twinged his conscience. He reached for the Book, intending to put it back on the side table, but instead he opened it absentmindedly. He read, *"For Adam was first formed, then Eve. And Adam was not deceived, but the woman being deceived, was in the transgression."* These words meant nothing to him, except to bring up a mental picture of a former biology teacher poking fun at the Bible in a lesson on evolution.

Mark closed the Bible, put it away, yawned, and picked up the *County Weekly*. He had not read the weekly paper in a long time. In the fall, he should be writing for the *Scranton Daily*; so he thought this a good time to get acquainted with what was happening in the surrounding counties. Among the stories about Wayne County political and social events Mark came across an unexpected thing. It was a limerick, of all things. He liked to dabble in that witty form of versification himself. He found limerick-writing punsters to be open-minded, intelligent. Most skeptics did. On the bottom of page five, there was a cartoon of two monkeys eating bananas on a tree limb. Mark read:

EVELUTION
Professor Ivan Simeaneve
Will give Science another reprieve.
"The way out," now he thinks,
Since he missed all the links,
"Is to call my chimps Adam and Eve."

While chuckling at the author's wit, his eyes fell on the name of the writer. He could hardly contain his surprise when he read under the quintet the name *Marco Nemo*. He read it twice, tempted not to believe his eyes. There could be no other Marco Nemo in the county. Mark would never have attributed a witty limerick to that man.

Mark was still lost in his thoughts when his mother came for him. She had been crying. "Mother would like to see you, Mark, before we leave." The thought occurred to Mark that one has to master fully the art of deception before shedding tears just to please somebody. Then the Bible verse he just read came to mind, *"...the woman being deceived, was in the transgression."* He shook his head and followed his mother into the corridor. They almost bumped into a petite nurse, her black, abundant hair contrasting with her white uniform.

"Abby!" Mark exclaimed in surprise. "So you are a…"

"—almost a nurse," the girl finished as she recognized the young man who had never heard the name Abigail before. "Let's see—you are Mark!"

"Yes. Mark. Mark Targett. With two *t*'s. At your service, as you probably expected to hear." He said the last few words without thinking that it might reveal a gentle mockery. He flushed. But the girl was not offended, though her wide grin told him she caught his unplanned derision.

"Mark Targett," she repeated sweetly. "I shall not forget the name if you don't mind my thinking of you as a hunter, not as a salesman. For 'a good marksman never misses his target' will help me remember your name."

"Abby, are you always so quick on the draw like this? And what do you mean you are almost a nurse? You look like a full one to me."

"Looks are deceiving, Mark". She sounded almost as if she was pontificating. Deception. Mark couldn't help thinking it odd that the thought should be popping up again. "I am only a student nurse being given the opportunity of practicing what I learn from books," Abby continued, "And I am being paid for that. Isn't that nice? You and your sister visiting some patient?"

"I am sorry I didn't introduce my 'sister' to you before." Mark was amused. "This is my mother, Helen, Dr. Carnegie. We just signed my grandmother in. Her doctor wants her here a few days for observation."

"Glad to meet you Mrs. Targett," Abby said, with a pleasant smile. No one felt the need to correct her. "Does the patient have the same name, Targett?"

"Yes, Grace Targett." Mrs. Cummings smiled.

I should be working with her. I'll be sure to take good care of your grandmother."

"Thank you, Abby," mother and son chorused.

"We might come across each other again. You two have a good day."

As she made a motion to leave, Mark found himself saying, again almost without thinking, "Abby, since I first met you with your grandfather's phone in your hands I have been wondering what else is there in your pretty head besides wit and puns. Would you allow me the privilege of picking your brain further sometime?"

Helen's presence made the girl feel safe. "There is not much there to be picked, Mark. You'll sure be disappointed. But you are welcome to it."

"Would you tell me when and where?"

"It has to be whenever you are not selling telephones

and I am not giving people baths," she replied, smiling. Our telephone number is in the book. Look under Swingle. Martha Swingle. That's my mom. Call when you can." She seemed to be in a hurry to get back to work.

"Thank you, Abby. I'll get back to you some time," he said, writing the name down on a card hastily fished out of his shirt pocket.

As Abigail Swingle left, Mark had the same sensation he had felt when she had walked out of his store. It seemed that here, too, the light went out of the carpeted hospital corridor where they had been standing for no longer than three minutes.

"Charming!" his mother breathed when the girl was out of hearing.

As the two were riding back in Mark's old sports car, Mark felt a little less estranged to his mother. She didn't look that old after all.

He thought of Abby then. Was Abby fatherless or did she have a father living somewhere else, as he did?

CHAPTER 8

Feminine Brutality

A whole week went by without Mark calling Abigail as he had initially intended. He had located the Swingle's telephone number, written on the back of his own Shaffer's sales representative card, and then hadn't called. He couldn't tell why. He finally had to admit that Abby both attracted and frightened him. How could a girl six inches shorter than he frighten him? She had given him enough evidence of being another Bible carrying religious "nut," yet was intelligent and vivacious. He ought to be cautious though. His chink was already too wide for safety and he should work at closing the gap, not willingly widen it.

He was uncertain as to why the girl attracted him. She definitely didn't fit the template he had in his mind for a female companion. Donna did. And so did other girls he knew who were as intelligent as Abby and prettier too. Abigail Swingle. A name taken straight from the Bible. Hadn't he read somewhere that Swingle is an Americanization of Zwingli, the name of the Swiss Protestant reformer? How many descendants did he boast in these parts? Maybe that should explain all the Bible names given to the towns around Honesdale: Bethany, Damascus,

Galilee, Nazareth, Canaan, Ariel…. He was glad that by fall he would be working in Scranton. He should find himself an apartment there and stay away from this 'sacred' area.

Could he be thinking of Abby because of Donna's letter? Her e-mail had been a long one. It must have been meant to make up for the length of time it took for her to answer him when he was trying to climb out of his "emotional mud hole" back at Christmas time. His old girl-friend had not been of any help. She had not reached for Mark's hand when he had called for help. She had let him fend for himself. He had gotten out without her help, or anyone else's, for that matter. He had dreaded hearing from her again, but he knew that it was inescapable.

The verbosity in the letter indicated hasty writing. After a neutral *"Dear Mark"* she launched into the subject of their relationship and on into her plans for herself, without any preamble. Just like Donna.

"Your call on Christmas Day sent me into a tizzy." she wrote. *"I had never heard you say 'I love you' to anybody and I never expected you to. Especially to me. As you often said, words are fickle things, unsuitable to express true reality. Their ineptness is unmistakable when dealing with abstracts, feelings. I learned those things from you, Mark, and I learned them well. Whoever or whatever writes the drama of life would have never written the phrase 'I love you' for Mark Targett to say. So, when I heard the words coming from your lips I didn't think you were yourself. Maybe you weren't, at least at that moment.*

"Whether it was a fluke or a permanent feature of a new Mark, my reaction to hearing you say it was logical, and, I think, what you expected my reaction to be. I had to be myself even if you were not, and react accordingly. I froze when I heard you express whatever feeling you needed to express at the time, with those trite words. My response was nil, not for lack of a suitable answer, but out

*of condescension to an actor who said the wrong lines...
and here we go, words, words, like you said, saying so little
for needing to say so much. And I with so many things to do
to help straighten out a world gone nuts and a nation going
backwards. But I must give a final word about love, whatever that four-letter word means. Do you remember telling
me how you reacted seeing your mother swooning while
listening to a crooner of the past singing 'Love Is Where
You Find It'? You and I laughed together about it. Love, an
idyllic, falsely guileless word as the term represented itself
in past years has acquired flesh and substance with our
sexual liberation. I remember saying to you: "Our generation thinks of alley cats when hearing the song "Love Is
Where You Find It" and are at home with the realism and
freedom the words express in this sense. The old generation
still thinks they can swoon in the moonlight when hearing
the same words sung but allow themselves to feel guilty if a
sensual thought intrudes in their sanctuary. I remember too
that you gave me high marks for having thus forced words,
especially the word love, to portray meanings more in tune
with the reality of our present stage of evolution.*

*"There was another silly song of the past about a guy
falling in love who said something stupid like 'I love you'.
Would you call me insensitive (a useful word in our political
correctness), or a sinner (in the useless vocabulary of the
past), if I say that that was you the other day? I still believe
that love is where you find it, whatever meaning for the
word people drag out of the past, fish out of the present pool
of meaning, or guess at in a more progressive future. That's
the best I can say, Mark, about our Christmas episode. To
have said to you 'I love you too, Mark', would have meant
nothing to me, to you or to anybody else, unless a few page
essay prefaced the confession. In the drama of my life, those
words are not in my lines as Donna Lindsay either.*

"Now for some more palpable subject. Since leaving the

university in Philly, I have given myself totally to the study of feminism. I am not an expert yet, but I am getting there. I have been very active here in Jacksonville as a member of Congressperson Simmons' staff. There's been talk about my being loaned to the staff of Senator Kerry as an investigative secretary. It has to do with his being viewed as one of the 2004 presidential candidates capable of beating our unfriendly Bush. (I had to put that in, Mark. You were always preaching at me for being too serious and challenging me to use more humor in talking or writing. Well, I am trying!) Being a diehard feminist and dead set on showing that my die is black, not pink, I'd rather see Hillary back in the White House. The position they call investigative secretary irks me, though. It smacks of something out of a capitalist playbook. But I shall take it as a challenge to spur me on to doing so much investigation that the Party would have to give me my own secretary or, better yet, secretaries. I am ambitious, Mark. You know it. You taught me to be ambitious.

By now, you know about the big rally in New York City for Feb. 14, Valentine's Day, of all things. I hope you are planning to be there. I am scheduled to be there myself. If you come, I promise to be your valentine for the day. Your old buddy, Shorham, will be speaking. I know how much you admire that comrade. After that, I shall go to Boston and stay there for as long as it takes me to fit into the 2004 presidential campaign groove. My final destination, as far as I can see ahead, is Washington, D.C.

"I understand that you have a few more credits to steal, borrow, or study for before society can officially call you a journalist. In my books you have always been one, and a good one at that. I still don't know where you are going or doing after that. If you continue to be a good boy, before long I might have some influence to spend on a childhood friend. Come to think of it, remember Prof. Knutsen? He always thought you were a star. He is already a member of

Kerry's team. Come on in, Mark. The water is warm, even though Massachusetts is not only the nation's land of the freer, but also the land of the cooler. You see, Mark, that I am trying to be funny. Just for you. I don't often succeed, I know, but I am trying really hard.

"Well, I am rambling. I am taking longer than expected in writing this. Sorry I didn't write any sooner. Not only is the sun always shining in Jacksonville, but also there are bright political things happening everywhere in town. I have been participating in as many politically correct activities as my unaccredited feminine strength allows me. And, believe me, I hardly have time to sleep. Or cook. I have so many luncheon meetings going on that I pretty much gave up cooking altogether. So, don't expect me to prepare for you your favorite dish (is it still Italian lasagna?) when you see me next.

Ciao,
Donna

The letter said more than Mark expected to hear. He knew his influence had been telling on Donna's personality. He had taught her to be assertive and independent. But not aggressive. The feminine brutality punching itself out of her was new to him. She had certainly not learned that from her teacher. Donna had astutely detected the chink in his armor but apparently never realized that loneliness was what cracked it. She seemed to be thinking that he had an out-of-character experience. Mark felt he had let her down. Was she going too far, too fast in the right direction to bring America in synch with the rest of the more cultured world? Just a couple of weeks ago Mark would not have averred that possibility in his friend's life and ideology. But he could not yet realize that of late he had been using a different scale to weigh things.

CHAPTER 9

Bookstore Prayers

Having Monday off, Mark thought it would be the right day to drive to the Borders bookstore. Senator John Kerry had written about his experience in Vietnam. In his book, he had not only the guts to buck the system and denounce America's atrocities in that war, but he had valiantly described them. Mark just had to read it. Political insiders kept talking about his intention of seeking the Presidency. Mark thought he had better bone up on the latest political scene too.

The bookstore was sold out of Kerry's book. Mark ordered one. It would take a couple of weeks. He decided to go to the coffee shop inside the store. There he would have access to the latest newspapers while sipping a good cup of coffee.

Mark was about to order his coffee when he saw her. Abigail Swingle, possibly the ten-far-removed-great grand-daughter of Zwingli, the Protestant leader who had given the Pope a run for his money... indulgence money, he added to himself, laughing. He could not remember where he had learned this piece of religious history. Abby sat at a table far from the coffee counter, engrossed in a book open before her.

Mark surprised himself by not hesitating to approach her.

"Hello, Gorgeous. Fancy meeting you here. Will I be stumbling on you everywhere I go for the rest of my life?" He was just trying to be funny, and Abby realized that. But she knew something else that Mark didn't know. Later he would find out that his breezy greeting was both fitting and out of place.

"Hi Mark Targett!" Abby responded, surprised too. "I wouldn't call it fancy, though. I'll have you know that I was praying for you just this morning."

Mark stared. The statement was simply outrageous. He felt unprepared to respond and could not hide his agitation.

"You what?" His wrinkled forehead and obvious perplexity were almost comical. Then he thought of the perfect retort. "I have heard they have saints in charge of all kinds of professions and situations. But I never heard of one patronizing TV salesmen or future journalists. When the saints marched in and out of earthly life, there were no TV sets or word processors. I am curious to find out which of the ones presently on duty in heaven you picked to bless me. What in the world did you pray for me, anyway?"

"What made you irritated by my telling you that I prayed for you this morning is precisely the reason and the objective for my doing it." Abby replied sincerely. "I have developed the habit of praying for whoever comes to my mind during my morning prayers. You came to mind while I was praying. It is as simple as that. I found myself thinking on what you said about finding out other things beside wit and pun lodging in my 'pretty head'. That was the second time you mentioned my looks. Usually girls like to hear they are pretty, especially when they are not. But it is not being honest. You were wrong in trying to deceive me and I wondered whether I brought it on in some way. I was certainly wrong in wishing I could believe what you said about my looks. That was what was in my mind just before I read the Bible text I had scheduled for me today. After reading it, I knew I had to pray for you. But I had to pray for myself first. To which saint did I address my petition on behalf of a certain Mark Targett? I know you are calling me a nut cake and I am about to give you one more reason for you to call me names. I like the idea of addressing God directly. I am that bold, Mark, in my nuttiness. There! Now you are smiling. It is much better that way."

But Mark's smile just covered the perplexity, which had returned during the girl's tirade, accompanied by a curious feeling. Had not this conversation with deception for a theme taken place before? Yet he knew Abby was just being her unthreatening self, that crispy, witty, sunny self he had never seen in any other girl.

He didn't know how to steer the conversation so he remained silent. Abby had not finished. Mark didn't know it, but he was not to be in charge of that conversation at all.

"Would you like to know what Bible verses guided me to pray for you after praying for myself?" Mark was not curious to know, but politely willing to humor her. Before he could answer his tormentor, she was saying in that honest, matter-of-fact tone of voice that always made her credible: "The words were addressed to a young man who was learning from the Apostle Paul the spiritual birds and bees of Christianity. My verses for today were, '*For Adam was first formed, then Eve. And Adam was not deceived, but the woman being deceived, was in the transgression.*'"

Abby noticed a startling change in Mark's countenance. There was bewilderment and a childish fear written on his face.

"Abby," he urged. "Let me see your Bible." She handed her open Bible to Mark with the verses highlighted and patiently waited. Mark looked eagerly for the words from the book he thought he hated, words that were twice in a week flung at him. He found them and read again the same words he read quite by chance in the hospital waiting room.

There was a long silence. Abby sensed she was not supposed to break it. At last Mark did so himself. "Abby, the Bible is a collection of many books, right?"

"Yes. The Bible is made up of many books put together."

"Do you know how many books?"

"Sixty-six".

More silence followed. Abby still waited. Again Mark spoke.

"Abby, I must go home now. I need to be alone. Will you meet with me again? Soon?"

"Of course, Mark. Let us pray you sell less TVs and I give fewer injections so we can meet again soon."

Mark responded with half a smile and stood up. Abby watched as the young man walked away. She didn't know what to pray for Mark as he found his way to the bookstore exit. But she did pray for him, anyway. Wordlessly. She didn't know what was in his mind. But she knew that something was afoot with his soul. And his soul was what she was after.

CHAPTER 10

A Request to Speak

Mark didn't go home after leaving Abby in the bookstore. He found himself vacillating in his emotions. He was trying to protect himself from specious feelings threatening to trespass his borders again. Home was where the latest break-in had occurred. Better not go there. Not yet. He drove to Scranton instead. He needed the company of likeminded people. He could not sort out his feelings of amazement from his recent conversation with Abby, and he was still smarting with Donna's stinging reproach.

The likeminded people he had in mind were acquaintances he had made while discussing his future in the offices of the *Scranton Daily*. The chief editor had introduced him to a couple of reporters on duty then. Mark hoped to plant a few seeds of friendship there. He needed the job for this coming fall. And he needed friends. As Donna reminded him, love is where you find it.

But the newspaper office was almost deserted, which was typical for that time of the day. Well, what now? He was hungry. Maybe he could find company at the Italian restaurant near the paper's premises. He hoped it was not too late for lasagna. He would have a glass of wine with his meal. He needed that too. Mark was bribing himself to maintain his guard.

There was just one other customer in the dining room: a portly man whom Mark guessed was Polish. The big man ignored Mark. Mark ignored him in return and ate alone. The glass of wine was an extravagance for him. He rarely drank liquor, but that was the only company he could think of. The lasagna was not fresh. The recently submitted heat from the microwave was still lingering on the pasta but had not rejuvenated the dish. The waitress looked tired, her unfriendliness hardly concealed by a professional smile.

Home and a book, Mark decreed to himself after paying the bill and reaching the street, still restless and unsettled. The old popular song Donna reminded him of in her caustic letter was insidiously running through his mind as he rode the new route 6. But, strangely enough, the word *home* replaced *love* in his mind. Home is where you find it. Mark wondered if there was any psychological force lurking behind his mind's rewriting of the song against his wishes. Words. One cannot trust them. And to think that he would spend his life putting them together for a living. They made good tools, readily available at the heart's entrance for emotions' use in order to break in. Mark stepped on the gas pedal. He was nearing Waymart, and the higher speed in a narrow stretch of the road would demand more of his attention. That was his goal.

His impersonal companions waited for him in his lonely apartment. If he was not feeling like reading, and now he wasn't, he had other company from which to choose. Radio, TV, and computer were obediently waiting to be awakened. He had again neglected to check his e-mail lately. He would see if there was anything interesting on the computer.

There was. Amongst the junk mail Mark downloaded was a newsletter from the student association at the university. It was about the coming rally in New York City that

Donna had mentioned in her letter.

Mark wondered why it had taken so long for him to become aware of the gathering. He ought to be more available to people of his own faith or lack thereof. He ought not to let the thought of Abigail intrude in his life too much. He wished he hadn't told her he would like to see her again soon. Why had he added the modifier soon to his already traitorous desire?

As he read the rest of his mail, Mark found out an even more interesting thing—he was wanted. There was a letter from the association's president attached to the announcement of the convention and addressed to him. The organizers needed a journalist-in-the-making to represent that profession in the gathering. Mark read that Professor Knutsen had suggested that his former student be chosen. The e-mail writer was sorry to be so late in notifying Mark of this. Things had been hectic on campus lately and he had overlooked the matter. Mark couldn't help thinking that this was not the reason for the president's neglect. He knew enough about the campus politics to know that there must have been some nay voters behind the delay. He wondered whether there had been some arm-twisting before they complied with the Professor's wishes. He wondered, too, whether Dr. Knutsen's choice of him had to do with Mark's journalistic potential or simply because the Professor still wanted to "go a long way with him." But at least someone was reaching out to him in his loneliness. And the distance made Mark feel safe.

Mark was invited to make a speech at the conference. Again, the e-mail writer was sorry not to have given him enough time to prepare his talk. But he had great confidence in Mark's writing and oratory skills. This feature of the convention was intended to help define the role of future journalists in the coming cultural war resurgence. The organizers wanted to challenge them to engage themselves in a more effective activism. They should be ready for the battles expected after the Nine-eleven thing died down.

Mark would accept the challenge. He would show Donna and Abby that he was still in charge of himself. He would write a speech that would break the barrier between his ideological and his illusory worlds. Emotions and nonsense must be weaned out of his world of illusion before he allowed it to mingle with his two other worlds. He would make them one in his own terms.

There was going to be a good side effect to the busyness of the next few days: Mark would have an excuse not to see Abby 'soon.' "I'll be busy until the fourteenth of February preparing a speech I'll be giving in New York City," he pictured himself telling Abby on the phone. He wondered what she would say then. She was good with comeuppance. There was no question about her saying something bright about his accomplishments. Mark had learned not to underestimate the girl.

Mark e-mailed his reply to the student association and to the committee. He would be glad to make a speech and represent the future unbiased journalists of the New America. Mark realized that he could not be an activist for a more socially conscious nation and be unbiased at the same time. But words worked well in league with duplicity. Their ineptness in portraying the substance of what they represented was a two-edged sword. Mark intended to become the best wordsmith in the business. Or should he say sword smith?

Mark was going to be off from work on Monday. Mr. Shaffer would let him be gone on Tuesday also, if needed, especially when he found out what his employee would be doing. Bob Shaffer seemed proud of his well-educated salesman. Mark reached for the phone and dialed Abby's number. There was no answer. He told his story on the answering machine after the beep. Abby would soon find out about his unexpected call to duty, and that it would take all his spare time until the fourteenth when he was due to be in New York City for a couple of days. Mark was pleased to be able to inform Abby of all that, but he wished she was going to be listening to himself, not to a machine. The impersonality of the communication robbed him of the satisfaction he anticipated in asserting himself before this mystifying girl. He would be missing the pleasure he derived from her surprising comments and clever repartees, for there was never a trace in Abby of that feminine arrogance when she exposed her witticism. That unbecoming trait he had observed in Donna and in other girls he knew. As for the feminine brutality, as he called it, that he had seen in Donna's letter—he knew that Abby would even recoil at the odd phrase. She would never hear the expression from Mark. He admitted to himself that he enjoyed the girl's company. He would miss not seeing her 'soon.' But he was ready to pay the right price for escaping the hook he kept seeing dangling at the end of the line, though unbeknown to her, whenever she was around.

Mark concentrated on what the rally organizers expected of him. What should be the contents of a speech about the role of young journalists in society in need of more enlightenment? He had great confidence in his ability to do a good job. Mark walked toward the shelves he had built in one of his apartment walls. They were heavy with his many books. He must write a clear outline first. While picking the books he needed for his material he felt great confidence in himself again. The threat to Mark Targett's wholeness was gone. And so was his loneliness. Mark Targett needed to be needed. But he didn't know how much yet.

CHAPTER 11

Library Probing

Mark and Abby saw each other sooner than they expected. It happened at the Honesdale Library. After writing the outline of his upcoming speech, Mark wanted to flesh it out with enough meat to satisfy his youthful hearers' appetite. He could think of a few books that would be useful in that. A dictionary of quotations is a good implement for intellectual cuisine purposes. The library should have one of those in its reference section. Mark had a passage in his speech where he would exalt the merits of modern education. He needed to quote Humes and John Dewey on the subject. He was happy to have Charles Francis Potter's *Humanism: A New Religion* handy in his apartment. His classic pronouncement had already been included—*"Education is thus a most powerful ally of Humanism, and every American public school is a school of Humanism."* (p. 128) But he still needed the reinforcement of John Dewey and Humes but could not find their books in his bookshelves. They must be among the many he had lent to Donna before she left Philadelphia. Should he write and ask her to bring them to New York with her? Perhaps he could find something in the local library. He didn't have time to go to Scranton.

It was unseasonably warm for early February. Mark noted with amusement some forsythia that had been fooled into putting out a few blossoms. Nature had been duped. Or nature duped itself, Mark mused as he turned down Main Street. He just could not understand why people would insist that God was in charge of what naturally occurred. Why would God busy Himself with little bushes in one tiny part of the world? It was ridiculous. Did people enjoy bondage to their belief that God was Creator? And why was it so hard for people to free themselves from the drudgery and nonsense of a God who was always a He? Mark remembered Donna's angry outburst when talking about this phantom male Being. What kind of a personality was this behind some mechanistic precision, this self-propelled carousel of unfailing repetitions? He ought to remember that rhetorical question when speaking next week in New York.

At the library, he found most of what he was looking for. The solicitous librarian guaranteed she would have a copy of the latest Humanist Manifesto on hand for Mark in a couple of days. For the time being he would spend some more time in the cozy reading room relishing a few more goods in the well-stocked library. He had hardly finished making himself comfortable at a desk when he felt a tap on his shoulder. Mark turned himself and saw more signs of a still undue spring. Abby stood there, girlish in her honest smile and long, colorful dress.

"My!" He said with exaggerated surprise, "What is such a gorgeous creature doing in a library on a day when the birds should be starting to think of working with their nests? You don't expect to give people baths in that finery, do you?"

Abby's merriment was obvious in her muffled laughter. "I am off today, you busy beaver. You don't really think I am on my way to give people their baths dressed like this! It is just that I felt I have been working and studying too hard lately. The sunshine sneaking through my window this morning woke me up and told me to spend the morning reading poetry. Robert Frost, my favorite. I have lent my Frost books to a friend. So, here I am. Of course, I had to dress in a way to celebrate the weather properly and to match my friend Frost's reverence of nature. And you? What are you doing here?

Mark felt he had to respond in kind to that exuberance. "You mean, what is a beaver doing out of the pond?" He smiled with a playful wickedness. "To use an image plaguing me all morning, I am preparing food for the banquet of ideas I'll be giving out next week in New York City. If you ask whether I like Frost I must say that he is not on the top of my list but I do enjoy his New England charm. The spring maid got my message the other day, I hope?" he asked, now serious.

"Yes, I did, Mark. Your tone of voice told me you seemed just too happy in not having to see me very soon as you threatened to do the other day. After your call, I should have known you would be a busy fellow this week. Maybe I should have borrowed Frost and gone home with the book when I saw you here, instead of charging in. Especially when you seemed to want to wiggle away from me. Now, here I am, an early spring bird pouncing on an innocent worm." She started her answer half-serious, but she was laughing again.

Mark was taken by the girl's humor. But didn't she realize that the real worm is the one someone tacked to the end of her fishing line without her knowing it? The enchanting creature didn't even know she had a fishing rod in her hands!

"No, Abby, I did not intend to avoid you," He lied. "It is just that this assignment is important to me. It can be a launching pad into the kind of life and activities I have been planning for myself all these years," Mark said soberly. "No, seeing you made this worm happy," he added, with a smile. "I think of you as a different kind of bird. You can't hurt a fly or gobble up worms. This worm doesn't feel threatened by you." He wasn't really too sure about that last statement. But Abby did seem to be harmless today.

The two had been talking in low voices so as not to bother the other readers in the room. It was so awkward to carry on a good conversation in whispers. Mark thought of taking Abby out to the car or somewhere and enjoying her company a little longer. He felt somewhat trapped, but it was a pleasant trap. He was about to do just that when he looked at his watch. In an hour, he had to be at work in the electronic store.

Abby saw Mark glance at his watch and she understood. "Mark, I wish you had the time to practice your speech on me. I am dying to hear what you have to say."

That took Mark by surprise. But he hid it well.

Half serious and half in jest he invited, "You can always come along and hear me in person at Columbia University." Then, just as quickly, "Come to think of it, you better not. There will be girls there who would shoot daggers at long-skirted Sunday school little girls who quote Bible verses."

"Really? Why they would do that? Would they take me for their enemy?"

"Nobody shoots daggers at friends, do they?"

"Little girls like me are afraid of handling daggers, Mark. But your friends don't scare me. I could quote for you a few Bible verses to show you why I'm not afraid of them. But the last time I quoted one for you, you ran away."

Abby's candid reply discomfited Mark. He couldn't find words to say. Then he thought, "Wouldn't this Bible-reading charmer be surprised with what she would be hearing if she came!" He decided he would give her a little taste of it. But not in person.

"Well, Abby," he nodded obligingly, "I have my outline completed. Here it is. And here are some coins. We'll make a copy of it in that machine." He pointed to the copier, "And you can take it home with you. P.S. Not to be read before or after ingesting Robert Frost."

"When shall I do it then?" Abby asked, mimicking Mark's firmness.

"That you'll have to find out for yourself, Curious George. Whenever you do it, try not to blacklist me altogether afterwards. Just keep my name and your relationship with me, from your job applications. And, Abby, promise not to read my outline before I reach the safety of home? I'd hate to see you react out of character for the girl I know as Abby." Mark exhibited seriousness, humor, and something close to poignancy in saying all this.

The copies were prepared in silence with the two of them waiting for the machine to spew out the warm printed pages. He handed them to Abby. She shook hands with Mark before leaving him. They never had shaken hands before. It was such an old-fashioned gesture, but somehow fitting.

"I'll see you when I come back from New York, Abby."

She waved, smiled, and was gone.

But he wondered whether Abby would still want to see him. The handshake she offered him could be significant. A handshake says more "Good-bye," than "See you soon." As Abby left the room, Mark felt that his self-confidence was leaving with her. He wished both of them would return. Very soon.

CHAPTER 12

Newspaper Appointment

Mark had subscribed to the *Scranton Daily* since Joe Colletti had introduced him to the paper's chief editor. That interview resulted in the promise of the job for the fall of the following year when there would be a vacancy in the writing staff. Mark's experience as a school paper editor had helped.

But much can happen in a year's time to change things. Since her conversion, his mother's friend could no longer be his job sponsor. Mark had been wondering, while working on his speech, whether he ought to keep closer contact with his future employer. He had not done much of that mostly for lack of appropriate occasions. The week before the convention in New York City, he found his opportunity to let the paper know that he was still interested in the job. He had just finished going over the outline for the talk when he picked up the daily newspaper from the Santilli's mailbox. He usually scanned the *Scranton Daily* in the morning. He took time to read only what interested him. That meant he never missed editorials or syndicated columnist's writings on national politics.

The paper printed a column by D. Javits, a political

commentator Mark admired. He found much food for thought in that morning's article. He used a couple of D. Javits' insights to add some validity to his forthcoming speech. They went well with the concepts Mark had in mind.

The help he got from the column prompted Mark to think up a way to keep in touch with the paper's bosses. He would not only let the newspaper know that he was still around, but add another star to his name. He called the paper before going to work. He still had the private number of Charles Scribner, the chief editor. All he had to do was find a way to get past his secretary. Mark remembered Mary Gallo from the interview she had arranged for him with Mr. Scribner. Would she remember him?

She did. And, yes, she would tell Mr. Scribner that Mark wanted his advice on the speech he was to give at the New York City Convention.

Twenty-five minutes later Mary called back.

"Mr. Scribner will see you tomorrow at nine o'clock, Mr. Targett. He'll be having an important meeting at ten; so please be here exactly at nine." She was all secretary. And a good one too.

At nine o'clock the next morning Mark was ushered into the plush office of the chief editor. Mr. Scribner stood up to greet Mark, shook his hand, and went right into the subject of the visit.

"So, you have been given the distinction of giving a speech on journalism before you are officially a journalist. Congratulations! My news editor just informed me about this youth convention in New York City. I have told him to find out the details from you. I want you to be sure and see Jabosky before you leave this morning. My secretary has already arranged for him to be available before you leave. Now, how can I help you?"

"Man of action," Mark told himself. This was going to be better than he expected. He had thought that the job promised him was a humble one. Maybe the paper would give him a better boost towards his goals than he had thought.

Mark got right to the point. "What I figure the organizers of the convention have in mind is to find out what are the thoughts in the minds of aspirants to journalism. Apparently, they judged me a good spokesman for them. I suspect, too, that how the young beginners in the profession and this year's graduates react to what I say should be of more importance to them than what I actually say. There is so much talk about biased reporting. We must be prepared to deal with this criticism. We ought to find new ways to get our message across without ruffling too many feathers. Of course, all I can come up with are ideas. You face the daily grind of putting a newspaper on the street rain or shine. I thought you could be a help in fleshing out my ideas or aborting them if they don't belong in the world of journalism. I'd like to give them more than they bargained for."

Mark had carefully prepared what he was going to say when faced with his power-wielding future boss. Now that he had delivered the first installment, he felt good about it. The chief editor received his words with a smile and a nod. That was a good sign.

"Fair enough, young man," the newspaperman replied, in a patronizing way that Mark recognized and abhorred. He continued, with hints of peer camaraderie. "You are guessing right about the organizers' intention. Your being already aware of the problems we face and seeing through the organizers' intention tell me that you are more than halfway in meeting their expectations. Are you aware of any effort to attract students and beginners of journalism to the convention?"

"Yes, sir. The project was advertised on various campuses in New York City and in adjacent areas. I am sure your local schools got the message. There were scholarships offered and full boarding for the three days. Some universities agreed to give credits to attendants. Some big names in the academic world are involved in this. I feel like a peon on a chess board."

The editor had to chuckle at this one, then, turning serious, "Looks like a newsy event. My news staff must have slept through its announcement. I thank you for filling me in. Something should be done, too, about the convention organizers choosing you as a speaker. That's good local news quality. Let us plan a write up on this." And following his words with action, he pressed his intercom button.

"Mary," he interjected, "please have Jabosky come to my office."

A few minutes later the news editor joined Mark and his boss. From then on all the talk centered on the projected story of the local boy making it good in New York City. The main reason for Mark's visit was almost forgotten.

After half an hour, Charles Scribner looked at his watch and hastily stood and blurted, "Got to go, fellows. You two finalize this thing. See ya." Then to Mark," You'll have to come back when I have more time for that fleshing out and aborting business. Call Mary about it."

Jabosky was clearly mystified at his employer's last remark. Mark almost laughed aloud at the look of amazement he flashed before regaining impassiveness. The chief editor sat down again, fumbled with some papers, picked up an envelope, and stopped the men just before Jabosky and Mark left the office.

"Mark," he said, still holding the envelope, "Before you go, I was just grappling with the decision on what to do with this letter to the editor item. I want you to read this. My secretary has the original copy. Tell me next time we get together whether as an editor you would print it or not. It is good subject matter for this fleshing out you expect. It's about getting our message out while avoiding bullets from the right. Of course, by the time we meet again I'd have made the actual decision myself. This is a test. This is only a test. Like the broadcasters say. I'll do all I can to help you discharge the responsibility you were given." He handed the envelope over to Mark and rose.

Mark could not talk long with Jabosky. He had to be back in Honesdale in half an hour. They made plans to meet again to write the story.

CHAPTER 13

Letter to the Editor

The envelope the chief editor of the Scranton newspaper gave to Mark remained unopened in his pocket until evening when he went home. There had been heavy customer traffic all day in the store. At home, about to eat a late meal, he retrieved the envelope. Inside was a four-page typewritten letter. It was addressed to the editor. Mark started to read the letter between gulps of food.

"Dear Editor:

"I have been an American by choice, not by birth, for nearly sixty years. I didn't come to America for what she can so generously give. I chose America for what she is. Before deciding to transfer my life, hopes and future progeny from my native country to America I studied this nation closely. I even taught myself her language in order to become satisfactorily acquainted with her. If asked to define this nation, the genius of America, the cradle from which she rose to greatness, here's what I would say.

"Over two hundred years ago the founders of America succeeded in designing for their budding nation the most fitting habitat for the humankind to live and thrive. Their

formula was simple: a small government with appropriate checks and balances, chosen from among the people, by the people; opportunities with incentives; and abundant freedom as the acting ingredient to make the formula workable. The recipe was found among sound Judeo-Christian tenets. This vital human diet had never been politically available to people anywhere, at any time in history. Word of such a marvel covered the globe. People from all over the world seeking to fulfill their humanity sensed the historical phenomenon taking place here. Like homing birds, they flocked to America's shores by the millions. While working to reach their personal goals they enriched their lives with meaning and built the greatest nation in the history of the world.

"I just read in your paper one of the latest columns D. Javits wrote—"

"So," Mark mused, "This is about D. Javits' weekly column the Scranton Daily published a few days ago." That was the same piece Mark raved about and whose insights he used in writing his speech. With this discovery, his interest in the letter increased. He was curious to find out what this scintillating writer had to say. Would he react positively to Mark's favorite columnist? He forgot to eat and concentrated on reading further.

"I have not missed many of that gentleman's columns, although the America he writes about is not the America I chose as home. Mine is an America whose authenticity cannot be erased from the facts inscribed on the rocks of reality by history's eyewitness scribes. D.Javits' understanding of America comes from modern editions of her history, revised to fit the philosophical theories of a few.

"I have been reading his columns regularly, intent on finding out how far he would go in senselessly blaming America for all wrongs. I believe this time he went further than I can quietly endure. To defend the motives and reasons

for the savage attack of Nine-eleven as pure and blaming America for herself attracting that inhuman deed is the height of absurdity. He has always rationalized into being absurd explanations for the maladies of the world. He doesn't seem to realize that the gates of freedom lead to both good and evil; that America's abundance of freedom brings about an abundance of both. Only truth in its state of exactness can intelligently distinguish between right and wrong. But truth for this columnist is what anyone thinks should be deemed as truth, as if, like beauty, it is to be defined by the eyes of the beholder. That is the only way the irrationality that has taken over D. Javits' writing talent can be acceptably explained.

"D. Javits is typical of the increasing number of Americans who blindly delight themselves in impugning America. It seems to be a credo accepted by the academia and the media that the socio-economic problems of the world have their source in this nation; that the problem of evil can be solved only by crusaders of good opposing America; that America has too many riches, too many weapons, too much technology for her own and the world's good. She must share all of that with a world that suffers simply for not having what she has. This giving sounds good and humanitarian—but is false, and reckless.

"No nation is a fitting sacrificial lamb for sin. The credo that the likes of D.Javits preach appeals to what is good in people's hearts without ever consulting their heads. And yet the mind is the only human organ capable of perceiving truth and truly understanding reality—that is if the exact measure of truth has not been discarded or tampered with. Good that comes from the heart alone can be disastrous to individuals, to families, to society, and to nations.

"In the absence of a mind with a true north, accusations are taken as guilt a priori. The secondhand guilt syndrome that is plaguing our nation, though unwarranted, is real. It

can only engender a good that is not appreciated, but considered as a due—and never charitable, because it is not. It is a good that invalidates incentives, stunts human and national growth, and robs people of human dignity. America became a great nation not by filling your bowl, but by providing you with all that is necessary for you to fill your bowl yourself. The America of entitlements instead of incentives and challenges is not the America whose perfect habitat for humankind her founders created.

"There is a reality about America which more and more people are being made to miss, a reality which adepts of relativism, man-centrism, and naturalism have been robbing from our citizenry. By dint of ideological aberrations the truths of the principles with which America was conceived has been taught as fiction in our schools for three generations. Though victims themselves, their graduates by their turn teach school; usurp legislative power while adjucating; control the media; get into the highest offices of the land; entertain the masses while teaching them their fallacious concept of America; and write books, newspaper editorials and syndicated columns. The true identity of America has been lost to them in their darkness. And, thus blinded, they insist on leading us into that darkness.

What those misinformed Americans learned from our misguided schools the world is learning from them. The lessons are being continuously transmitted around the globe via our ingeniously built communication highways. The world community is being taught the same hate-eliciting misconceptions about America that are being steadily drilled into us here at home. They want the real America to die so that what she owns for being what she really is can become common property without a price to pay. Many want to expedite America's death by destroying her with their own hands.

"What this all means is that another America, one her

fathers never conceived, is being gestated within the old one. Because we still practice democracy and, unlike D. Javits' chameleon-like truth, numbers are inflexible in their absoluteness, the Pilgrims' America is being slated to die giving birth to 'The Other America'...."

At this point in Mark's reading, he shuffled through to the end to find the writer's name. As he was starting to suspect, the letter was signed: Marco Nemo. All the time Mark had been reading the letter he had kept his mental fists ready to hit the invisible writer. But what he saw before him was the heaving back of an old, foreign-born man calling America "his America." And between Marco and him stood another gentle, sensitive old man. Mark would never strike Papa. Even if Papa wrote that letter himself. It was with a mind in turmoil, his heart divided, that Mark went back to reading the rest of Nemo's letter.

"For over half a century I have hoped against hope that D. Javits and all the misled Americans they represent would come to their senses. That those who love this country would realize that America could overcome her many enemies within and without her only if armed with her identity. Only in the real America can be found the means her wise conceivers provided her with for her survival in a world plagued with crisis and catastrophes, even when crisis and catastrophes not of her making cross her borders.

"I know that the length and content of this letter make it unprintable. But I had to take this heavy weight off my America-loving chest. Thank you for listening. And God bless, my friend. God bless.

Marco Nemo"

CHAPTER 14

Grandmother's Need

The week was turning out to be a busy one for Mark. It was a good thing he had the speech already written. The new encounter with the chief editor didn't yield much to his speech. But Scribner had learned a few more good things about his future reporter. Then there would be the write-up for Mark's accomplishments. The *Scranton Daily* editor decided to wait until the New York youth convention was over before telling the story of the local boy making good in New York. He would combine a write up on the New York convention with Mark's role in it. Yes, he was on his way to enter in the path he had chosen for his life.

As for Marco Nemo's letter, there was no chance of it being printed, just as Mark expected. The exchange he had later with the chief editor on that matter was brief. The question to print or not to print was, really, academic. Mark's requested opinion on the matter, when expressed, just gave Mr. Scribner the opportunity to make a dubious contribution to Mark's already finished speech. Mark found it distasteful.

"If shots from the right are coming from BB guns or bullets from small arms," the chief editor instructed, "you print the thing and get it over with, and you count it as another weight on the scale of fairness. If you recognized the barrage to be coming from a sophisticated weapon, you ignore it. This Nemo, Bembo, or whatever this guy's name is, is probably a malcontent left over from the European dwindling aristocracy, trying to make a name for himself. I bet you he has written a book that nobody wants to print. When you don't succeed in the big city, you try to start scaling the ladder from the smaller towns. I am not about to give the guy a hand."

Mark found Scribner's remarks sardonic. His barbs hit Mark too. Wasn't he also starting with a humble hack job in a smaller town? Mark concluded that the editor was not a sensitive man. He would have to keep that in mind when working there. He never revealed to Scribner that he knew who the writer of the letter was and that the editor was as mistaken as he could be about Marco Nemo. The old man he last saw holding a Bible under his arm was definitely not European. And he was no leftover from the aristocracy either.

Mark had to admit that he had his own faults. He had not intended to get any help from Scribner to write his speech. He only wanted to use the occasion to remind his future employer that he was still around. His deception had paid off handsomely. Mark was too honest not to feel a twinge of guilt. But he assured himself that for the sake of his coming career he would have to get used to some duplicity.

Mark was reminiscing about these things in his apartment on Sunday morning when the telephone rang. It was Granny Targett. Mark could not remember the last time she had called him. They didn't talk much with each other. Her voice sounded weaker than he remembered. As mother said, Granny was not well.

"Mark, dear," she started, "I need to bother you again."

"Whatever it is, Granny, it can't be a bother. How are you feeling?"

"Thank you, Mark. As good as can be expected, But your mother has convinced me that I should move in with her so she can take better care of me, as she puts it. I wouldn't have thought of ever agreeing with this. Living together with someone who is already an adult is not easy, even if it is your own child. But Helen has changed, Mark. I am sure I'll enjoy her company and care as I live my last days." Grace Targett stopped to catch her breath.

"What will you be doing with the house then, Granny?"

"I'll have to sell it. I might be needing extensive medical care before long. This could prove too much for Helen then. I should be prepared to move from your mother's to some health care facility somewhere. The house is already registered with realtors. Mark...," her pleading tone of voice saddened Mark.

"Yes, Granny...."

"May I ask you to help me manage this big move? I tire easily and my mind keeps playing tricks on me. Your mother is willing to help and has been good to me, more so since she began to change. Actually, I don't know what I would have done without her, especially since my medical condition worsened. You know your mother has had some kind of religious experience, don't you? She seems like another person. But we need a man to help us. Not just to move furniture and things. We need a man's mind on which to bounce our ideas and decisions. And we could use your advice. Besides, I miss seeing you, Mark."

There was another pause during which Mark squirmed under the pricking of his conscience reminding him that he had not been the kind of devoted grandchild he was supposed to be. He decided then and there to visit Granny often and make up for his dereliction. He would do the same with his mother too. And that would give him the opportunity to confirm first hand the change in her of which Granny was certain. He himself had seen something different in her.

But, then, Mark was a skeptic, and proud of it.

"Granny," he said. "I just finished breakfast. Let me drive right over and we can see the size of the job ahead and talk about it."

"Thank you, Mark. I really appreciate it. But I had planned to be in church this morning. This is important to me. Come for dinner if you can. Your mother is coming too, and I'll be preparing chicken and rice for us. There will be enough for you too. What do you say?"

Church? It didn't sound like Grandmother Targett. Had she gotten religion also? Shaking his head, Mark made a quick decision. That day happened to be one of the monthly Sundays when he didn't have to go to the store at one o'clock. He had other plans for his day off, but he would scrub them and do what seemed right.

"That's a deal, Granny. What time do you need me there?"

"Make it one o'clock. That will give Helen and me time to set things up. The church is not far and should be over at twelve."

"I will be there! And, Granny..."

"Yes, Mark."

"I am glad you called. It will be good to see you!"

Was Mark changing? He certainly hadn't cared much for these women in his life before. Change could be a good thing. As for getting religion, well, not much of a chance there.

The weather condition was not cooperating, but that was not going to keep him from doing what he felt he should do. His faithful old front wheel drive buggy would bring him back safely, whatever the skies delivered.

CHAPTER 15

Abby's Gratitude

Abby and her mother lived in a little house half a mile past the village of Bethany's small park. A Methodist church and a library were the most outstanding buildings among the few houses. The snow covered their well-cared-for lawns. It would be many weeks before the greens of the many trees gracing the old burg would add more colors to the scene. Flowers from the gardens and the park would soon be helping make the little village seem enchanted again.

Martha Swingle was petite like her daughter and, like Abby, quick of movements and mind. She could easily be taken for Abby's sister though she was in her forties. She had never remarried after she was widowed when Abby was nine. She had loved Gary Swingle deeply and still had a great capacity to love, but she was content in spending it on God, her godly parents, and her look-alike daughter. There was still much love left in the reservoir of her heart for other good things. Her country, people, flowers, and a little mutt who thought he was the most important member of the family.

She and Gary had started dating each other in high school. Reared in the fear of God, both of them felt out of place in a school atmosphere heavily influenced by the looseness of the times. The two felt nobody, especially the young and inexperienced, should be in a place where God was forbidden. Their shared perception caused them to cling to each other during the difficult teenage years in high school. The closeness only intensified after marriage.

When their love blossomed into fruit and Abby was born, they decided they would homeschool the child. What convinced them of the wisdom of their decision was the experience they both had had in college. Martha had taken biology with a view to teaching the subject. Gary went for pilot's training with the Navy. What they witnessed about the direction the nation's education system was taking convinced them that they should not let government schools mold their children's minds.

They started homeschooling Abby early. Then Gary was sent to the Middle East to fight. After he died, Martha continued Abby's lessons alone. It was nearly an impossible task while carrying the enormous grief of her loss. But her father took Gary's place. He proved to be an influence on the child for which Martha would be grateful all of her life. Abby turned out to be as keen minded and as godly as her Pappy, as Abby affectionately called him.

This morning Abby had been spending more time than usual in her morning devotions. Martha was not teaching school today. She was busy in the kitchen, preparing breakfast for both of them. Burt, the canine member of the family, already had had his. He had curled up next to Abby's feet. The girl suddenly stood up quickly and ran to the kitchen. The dog jumped too, startled at Abby's fast movement. Abby laughed at the dog's jerking but didn't have the time to assure him that all was well. She called—"Mother! Mother!" Finding her mother at the sink, she impulsively hugged her from behind as she exclaimed, "Oh! Mother! Thank you, thank you!"

"What's all this about, child?"

"I just realized the depth of the big hole you saved me from by homeschooling me." Martha dried her hands on a towel and turned to her enthusiastic daughter. Abby continued, "You and Pappy have told me often what is happening in our nation's schools. But now I see it at a much closer range. This poor Mark Targett! Such a brilliant mind led to seek meaning for life in the dark! This outline of the speech he'll be giving in this youth convention, Mom, is a summary of what you and Pappy have been telling me can happen to young people's minds in our schools today. Mark has been taught to believe that there's nothing solid and permanent on which to rest his soul. No surety. Nothing real except what he can touch. Our parents—the past—have nothing to offer a generation supposedly in a higher state of mental evolution. God is a myth. What a terrible burden life must be to young people like Mark. No wonder thousands of them kill themselves and millions are forfeiting their lives in exchange for quick pleasure. Oh! Mother! Only God knows what you and my dear Grandfather have kept me from! What Mark's education has done for him was to usher him into a chaotic world with a baseless hope of human society becoming a secular paradise."

While seated at the table and even after grace, Abby went on excitedly, "And this is to be done strictly through politics and education. That entails keeping the notions of God, traditional families, and the Bible out of the way. These things are considered as hindrances to the evolutionary process. Mark's world is a world without constancy or consistency. He reminds me of a space vehicle in a wrong re-entry angle, bouncing off our atmosphere and condemned to go round and round in space forever. Or else burning up as it plunges through the atmosphere. Can you imagine, Mother, having nothing sure to base your decisions on because there is no exact standard to give stability to life and society? Not even to distinguish right from wrong, good from evil? They don't even want to think of a man as a man and a woman as a woman. Something called personhood has banned even that natural distinction."

Mother and daughter finished breakfast in thoughtful silence. Suddenly Abby asked, "Mother, have we mailed the valentine card we bought for Pastor yet?"

"No, we haven't. That's one thing I plan to do this morning."

"Can I have that one, Mother? We'll find another for him. I would like to send that one to Mark."

"If you feel that you should, go right ahead, Abby." Martha picked up the card from the desk of her little office by the kitchen and brought it to the kitchen table.

Abby opened it and smiled broadly. "You know, Mother, when Mark made a copy of his detailed outline for me to read he said something revealing. He said that the young people he will be with in New York consider me their enemy. They hate Sunday School girls with long skirts who quote Bible verses. Before praying for Mark this morning I read a verse that tells me exactly how to react to that." She picked up the Bible resting on the kitchen table where Mother had her morning prayers.

Finding the passage, she said, "Here it is. *'If thine enemy be hungry, give him bread to eat; and if he be thirsty, give him water to drink: For thou shalt heap coals of fire upon his head, and the LORD shall reward thee.'* Coals of fire in the Bible signify purification, as you know. And Mother, that was my Old Testament text for the day. The New Testament one is exactly the verse printed on the card we bought for Pastor Brown. How's that for guidance?"

Abby wrote what she wanted to add to the valentine card and addressed the envelope with her brisk steady handwriting. "There," she added, smiling, "What do you say we pray now that the coal doesn't burn that knuckle head, but just purifies those awful thoughts inside of it?"

CHAPTER 16

The *County Weekly*

⁓⦾⦾⦾⁓

Early Sunday afternoon Mark drove up the country road leading to Grandmother Targett's under a threatening sky. He had not followed the weatherman's predictions lately and hoped they were not in for a blizzard. He didn't think much of being snowbound in Granny's house with his mother there saying pleasant things she might not mean. Besides, he promised Mr. Shaffer he would be at work Monday morning even though by the books it was his day off. Mark might need extra days free next week for the convention.

It had been a long time since he last visited Grandmother Targett. He had no explanation for this neglect. The driveway of her house was clear. But the old snow of former storms was still piled, unmelted, everywhere. They showed the brownish streaks made by the salted mud tossed by car tires. Mark wondered who shoveled the driveway for the old lady. She could not certainly do it herself and his mother couldn't be around all the time to do it. Wasn't that something he could easily do for Papa's wife? His growing sense of guilt appeared in his chest as a heavy sigh. He parked his car behind mother's blue Camry. The air outside seemed conditioned for a snowstorm.

Mark saw the two ladies in the kitchen when he opened

the front door after hearing a musical "Please come in, Mark!" in response to his ringing of the bell. It was his mother's voice. Granny could have never heard the soft ringing the bell made. His mother was right. Granny Targett should not be alone anymore.

"Make yourself at home, Mark," this time from Granny. "We'll be bringing the food into the dining room in a few minutes."

The table was already set. Grandmother was using her old, expensive china she reserved for important guests. He swallowed hard again, then returned to the vestibule where sat an ancient coffee table. He remembered that piece of furniture, but it was out of place. Books were piled up on it. Granny must be moving things around already. On top of the bulky family Bible, he saw a copy of the *County Weekly*. Mark picked it up. He hadn't read the county's paper since he took Granny to the hospital a few weeks before. Did they still print Marco Nemo's limericks? He walked to the living room while opening the weekly paper. It was the latest one. Mark found what he was looking for on the top right of page five. THE WEEK'S LIMERICK, he read. The words were printed in capital letters over a cartoon picture portraying a typical South American man. "So it is a regular feature now," Mark thought, recalling the *Scranton Daily* chief editor's words about failing book writers seeking minor publications as stepstools. Mark could not picture Marco Nemo as one of them. It was probably a hobby that the editor had suggested he share with his readers.

"*Excuses, Excuses!*" was the title of the limerick.

Tio Sam, I would like to pay back
That old loan, but my country is a wreck.
Our bananas got rot,
Our drug dealers got caught,
And my Swiss bank account gives no check.

"Definitely not politically correct," Mark chuckled. "But the old man does have a sense of humor. Maybe Bible-carrying Christians are not as bad as we think. Abby is certainly witty. How she holds on to that Bible of hers! She's supposed to read it through once every year, I hear! What is in that ancient book to interest old men on their last leg and bright young kids like Abby? Maybe I ought to find out—"

Mark's thoughts were interrupted by a call from the kitchen, "Come and get it!" a trite expression Mark no longer enjoyed. He remembered hearing that while he and Papa waited in the living room for Granny to lay the Sunday dinner on the table. That time with Papa was dear. He would read to him, or arm wrestle with him before he became sick. He always tried to answer Mark's many questions. There had never been a grandfather like Papa.

They placed Mark at the head of the table. Would they ask him to say grace?

"You look good, Mark," Granny commented after Helen helped her to her seat. Mark had not even thought of doing that. He remembered how Papa always helped Granny sit. Mother went around him and sat at his right.

"We now say grace before we eat, Mark," she said. And then she prayed, reverently. He didn't really listen. Why did Mother sound apologetic about praying before eating?

The conversation around the table was mostly on generalities. They inquired about Mark's future projects, how he was doing in his work and in school, and whether he was happy living alone in an apartment. They seemed to be interested. But his answers were restrained. He wasn't pleased with the talk about himself. He couldn't help but notice that his mother was not agreeing with him even before he finished what he was saying.

Before they finished eating the snow had whitened the fields. Mark still hoped the roads wouldn't become impassable before he had to go back. The food was good, as he always remembered Granny's cooking to be. Mark was just finishing his apple pie when he asked, "Granny, do you always read the *County Weekly*?" He had noticed that her name and address were labeled on the front page of the copy he had before dinner.

"Yes I do, Mark," she answered, "Mostly to find out what is happening to people and families I know in the county. That's one of the main features of the paper, you know. It is the way I find out news on marriages, births, and deaths. Old folks like to keep informed about people. And I never throw the paper away either."

"You keep every one of them, Granny? Why do you have to do that?" Mark wanted to know.

"It will surprise you to know why I keep them. I do it for you, Mark."

"For me?" Mark asked in disbelief, "Why are you keeping the *County Weekly* for me, Granny? I'll never—"

"Because I have always known that you'd be a writer. When writers get old they like to write about people and their past. I know. I was married to one for thirty-five years. Writers have better and easier access to information about people and events if they have the original source on hand. This way they don't have to spend time in research. And time, Mark, is very precious when you have little of it left."

Mark was moved. "Grandmother does care for me," he thought. "I never suspected it. Where have I been all these years?"

"Weeklies are not difficult to store, you know," She continued. "It is not like daily papers. I have every one of them since they started publishing them years ago. You cannot keep them in an apartment. But you'll have a house someday, Mark. A big house with plenty of light and a comfortable writing studio. That's what your Papa would have had by now if he had lived long enough. You are just like your Papa, Mark. He had great plans for the future and his plans always involved you. I know that you will carry out his dreams. You'll be able to finish what he started."

"Oh, Granny! Why have you kept all this from me all these years? I never—"

"You have been too busy chasing dragons since you started school, Mark." Grace continued as if she had not been interrupted. "I have been waiting for you to come back from your crusading foray. You are not back yet, but you will be some day. I just hope I stay alive long enough to see that day. It will be as if my own Mark Targett had come back home."

The old lady dried stubborn tears from her wrinkled face during the ensuing silence. Mark was finding it difficult to keep to the emotional diet he had prescribed for himself. Guilt had been stealing on him since Grandmother called on the phone this morning. That and this new revelation could push him over the limit he had set up for himself. Had his Grandmother known all the time how he longed to be like Papa? "Watch now, living Mark Targett!" he told himself. "The dam is about to break and you are not ready yet for this to happen!"

Mark swallowed hard, then murmured, "I shall not disappoint you, Granny. You'll see." Then, humorously firm, "Now this Saint George is ready to start planning your big move. When can we start?" Mark said, wittingly, with half a smile. Practicality was a cover up and he knew it. So did Grace Targett.

All during the interchange between him and Grandmother, Helen had just sat there, unusually silent. Finally, she said, "We are so grateful, Mark, that you are willing to help. We were worried sick about having to cope with moving by ourselves."

From this point on the conversation dealt only with the business at hand. There were the questions of a date for the move, storage space rental for the items that would not fit in

Helen's house, the selling of some, the packing, the need for another pair of man's hands. It was not going to be an easy job. Not an easy transition for Grandmother Targett either. But she was being very brave and held her own. She was able to have her say in the planning.

By now, the snow was falling thick and fast. Mark suggested they survey the house to see all that needed to be moved out. He helped the two ladies clear the table and then they got started.

They went through the whole house, Granny Targett moving slowly and feebly. As they surveyed the house, they talked. Mark remembered some of the things he grew up with when they filled the old farmhouse in upstate New York. What he couldn't remember, Grace Targett described to him. The only place where she couldn't go was the attic. Most of the old things were stored there.

Mark and his mother climbed into the attic together. Everything was neatly placed and cared for. Mark could see his mother's hands in this. Granny couldn't have done it all by herself.

At the entrance of the attic, easily reachable while the climber was still halfway up, was Granny Targett's collection of the *County Weekly*. The piles were covered with thick, transparent plastic. As she had said, they didn't need much storage space. Mark wondered what he would do when he inherited them. He was a forward-looking 21st Century "dragon-chaser" as Granny had put it. The past had not much to teach. Was he being a false pleaser like his mother used to be? He had told Granny that he would not disappoint her, but he might have to.

By the time they finished the survey and made most of the decisions, the snow outside was piled high and was still falling. They turned the TV on. The first thing they heard was a storm advisory. Twelve inches of snow was expected to be followed by sleet. They were warning that vehicles were not to be on the roads until the snowplows had done their job. "It is going to be a long night," the weatherman opined. Mark and his mother knew that they would have to buckle down and spend the night in Granny's house. Their cars were not garaged. They were already partly buried in snow.

Though the house was small, there was enough room to accommodate them for the night. The two ladies went to bed early. Mark stayed in the living room, watching the TV to keep up with the weather situation in between other news. Something in the local news reminded him of Granny Targett's collection of the county's paper. Would he be able to find there something about the Swingle clan? Mark still knew little about them. He had to kill time. Why not? He climbed again to the attic. It was cold there and he didn't want to linger. He picked up the first pile of papers he found accessible and brought it down the stairs. He wiped off the little dust on top of the pile and untied the string holding the papers together. They were ten years old. There were a few news items about various Swingles. He scanned the papers for more. They were placed in chronological order.

In the one for the first week of May, he came across an item that paid off. Under the heading, *"Local Airman Shot Down Near Kuwait"* was a picture of a young Navy pilot with the caption: *"Lt. Gary Swingle."* The article was brief and to the point—a local Navy jet pilot was shot down over the Persian Gulf while on a reconnaissance mission on August 10. Observers reported his jet crashed before the pilot could eject from the spiraling aircraft. Navy officials confirmed his death. Data about the downed pilot followed the dry announcement. He was a 1980 graduate from the Lake Ariel High School, had joined the Navy Flight School immediately after graduation, and received his wings three years later. He was assigned to the aircraft carrier Eisenhower on duty in the Persian Gulf. *"Lt. Swingle is survived by Martha Swingle, of Bethany, and a daughter, Abigail Swingle."*

Mark spent a long time in his grandmother's living room trying to fit together this tragedy in the past of the strange girl that occupied his mind so much lately. Why hadn't she ever mentioned it? Had Abby's mother remarried? Mark realized he knew little about this lively young girl's life. Yet, the little he knew about her had already affected him, in a pleasant way.

Mark dreamed about Abby during the night. In his dreams were crashing planes and pretty girls in long dresses with Bibles in their hands. Papa made a few cameo appearances, strangely enough, also with a black Bible in his hand.

Abigail Swingle, daughter of dead Navy Pilot Gary Swingle was still very much in his mind as he dug the two cars out of a foot of snow in the driveway at seven o' clock in the morning.

CHAPTER 17

The Speech

M ark was not about to take his little sports car to Manhattan. He once had it stolen in downtown Philadelphia. The police were able to find it and restore the CRX to him after a few days, but with some bangs and lots of dirt. It had cost Mark money and aggravation. He decided to ride on the bus that connected Honesdale to New York; then take the subway to uptown Manhattan for the main campus of Columbia University where he was to stay at the university's guesthouse.

Mark took the morning bus. It was Wednesday. The convention had started the day before, but Mark didn't want to let Mr. Shaffer operate the place without him. He wasn't due to speak until Wednesday evening anyway.

His change of clothes and his toiletries were in a valise he had used since his early high school days. Mark was conservative when it came to possessions. His car was almost as old as he was. In an attaché case, he had a couple of books, his written speech, and the mail he picked up last night but hadn't had time to read.

The bus left on time. Mark sat next to a thin quiet man who had no inclination to talk, thankfully. It had been years since he had ridden in a bus. He made himself comfortable, opened the attaché case, and took out his mail. It was mostly advertisements—two of them from jewelry stores persuading him to buy his valentine present there. The other two vied for his telephone business. "Capitalism," he thought. "Rank capitalism. And to think that the customer has to pay for the cost of the bait business men throw at him!"

He would like to see what the alternative plan for the distribution of goods would do to Wall Street and Madison Avenue. The system he had learned was better was generally in books only. Granted, it had been tried in other countries and the result was not good. But those were countries where there was nothing much to be distributed. It couldn't fail in the richest, most productive nation in the world. After Roosevelt, its defenders had managed to gain some of the ground which capitalism had been holding for years. Those opposed to socialism complained about how the meager tokens of wealth distribution were "bloating" the government. Marco Nemo had written in his letter to the editor that small government had helped to make America a rich country. Where had the old man got that idea? In his speech, Mark touched on the subject, challenging future journalists to find new ways, new expressions, to get the people to understand the issues. The education system was doing a good job in freeing students from the capitalistic jingles they heard all the time. Uneducated people had only the media to teach them about the importance of opposing big business. Unhappily, the media depended on commercial ads. That was another difficult job for future journalists— finding ways to be independent of money doled out by the status quo. "It is going to be a good speech," Mark assured himself as the GMC liner took him swiftly and in comfort to the big city.

All the while he was musing over the ideas his mail had sparked, he was holding a handwritten envelope in his hand.

He had forgotten about it, enmeshed in the economic issues that would yet break America or keep her strong. He turned over the envelope to study it. On the top left was the address of the sender, but no name. Mark's name and address were written in bold, round letters, in a style unmistakably feminine. "Ah! What have we got here? A valentine card!" Mark was not interested in any moneymaking scheme capitalism had dreamed up to draw the cash flow. Valentine Day ranked next to Christmas Day in his unwanted list. But he opened the envelope anyway.

It was from Abby. Mark was glad to find out it was not the usual mushy valentine card. It showed writing in Gothic style with classic calligraphic adornments tastefully done in gold. There was a quotation. From the Bible of course. It had to be, coming from that girl. Mark purposely ignored what the verse said and concentrated on the handwritten note. Even if she had not signed it, it would have still shown the earmark of Abby. She wrote *"To a new friend who shall not escape her friendship by shielding himself with the companions he thinks are her enemies."*

"That kid!" Mark whispered to himself. "She never fails to surprise me!" He mulled over Abby's words before bravely reading the Bible verse Abby had picked for him: *"Greater love hath no man than this, that a man lay down his life for his friends."*

Abby's bold words and the Bible text occupied his mind as the bus rode by Lake Wallenpaupack. Mark's thoughts raced, "Her words are clearly a reference to our interchange a few days before in the Honesdale Library. But she made sure to mention in this card that I thought my companions were her enemies, not she. What meaning should I attach to this? You can never be too careful with that girl. And did I indicate to her that I was trying to escape from her, or is this just feminine rhetoric? But there's no mistaking what she means by my shielding myself. I know this is true. Indeed, I do fear her and her people. But how does she know? I fear that they might usher me into an Illusory World different from the one I am already a part of. The truth is I do delight in her company. But there is a price to pay to have her company instead of the company of 'her enemies'. And why do this girl, Marco Nemo, and my reformed mother keep reminding me of Papa? Had he been a part of this Christian cabal? Was sorcery behind Bible-quoting people who show sensitivity and more awareness of others than most? Calm down now, Mark Targett. Papa was not a Bible nut even though he comes to mind when Abby calls your name. You are safe, dragon chaser! You don't have to shield yourself behind Abby's enemies. Just watch for Abby herself. She doesn't know the power she has to drag you kicking and screaming into the make-believe world she and Marco Nemo belong to."

It was a long time before Mark could open an old back issue of The Humanist magazine he had secured when just finishing high school. Mark couldn't remember how he came to own the old periodical. He couldn't have bought it new. It was printed before he was born. He turned resolutely to the 1976 copy he had with him. A quotation of something he remembered reading in it would enhance his talk. It didn't take him long to find the quote he remembered from his high school days:

Something wonderful, free, unheralded, and of signif-icance to all humanists is happening in the secondary schools. It is the adolescent literature movement. They may burn Slaughterhouse Five in North Dakota and ban a number of innocuous books in Kanawah County, but thank God the crazies don't do all that much reading. If they did, they'd find that they have already been defeated. Adolescent literature has opened Pandora's box. . . nothing that is part of contemporary life is taboo in this genre, and any valid piece of writing that helps to make the world more knowable to young people serves an important humanistic function. (January/February, 1976)

That seemed written for today, Mark concluded. He felt it was fitting indeed to be included in an address to future writers. He took his written speech out of the attaché case and looked for the place where this quote could do the most good. He decided that it belonged with the paragraphs mentioning the great changes that had taken place in American education since John Dewey, but could not decide whether to place it before or after the other quotes from university professors in charge of training future teachers. Mark read them again to figure out just where:

Every child in America entering school at the age of five is mentally ill because he comes to school with certain allegiances toward our founding fathers, toward our elected officials, toward his parents, toward a belief in a supernatural Being, toward the sovereignty of this nation as a separate entity.

It is up to you teachers to make all of these sick children well by creating the international children of the future. (Professor of Education and Psychiatry at Harvard University, given at a childhood education seminar in 1973, reaffirmed in 1983)

"That's powerful stuff," Mark thought. "A good introduction to what follows: *'The classroom must and will become the arena of conflict between the old and the new— the rotten corpse of Christianity . . . and the new faith of Humanism.'*" ("A Religion for a New Age," The Humanist,

January/February 1983, p.26)

And then Julian Huxley in the UNESCO Manual for our children's education approved by an American President wrote, *"(The Manual)... is to provide the foundation upon which international government must be based... The kindergarten or infant school has a significant part to play in the child's education... it is frequently the family that infects the child with nationalism."*

Mark remembered that he had attached the last two quotes to the outline of the speech he gave to Abby. Was he being too hard on the poor kid? That could surely justify that enemy bit.

Mark decided to place the new quotations after the others. He reasoned that next he'd be talking about the need for journalists to understand the job of modern teachers. This understanding should foster more of a teamwork mentality between teachers and journalists. The daily newspapers' reading material should always accord with the reformed school classes.

By the time the bus crossed the George Washington Bridge, Mark pronounced his work complete and himself ready—ready to perform his duties as a citizen of his Ideological World.

Then, out of nowhere, the picture of Marco Nemo and his America came to his mind. It was a preposterous recollection at that juncture. Mark wished he could restrict that memory to the village of Canaan.

CHAPTER 18

Idealism Shattered

America's big cities are, in the court of reason, concrete evidence that freedom is a gate opening up into both good and evil. They are the litmus test of a nation's belief in freedom and of her survivorship. New York City is exhibit number one. The ugly gap in her skyscape where once the two proud towers stood left no doubt that the metaphor was more than just a figure of speech.

Time Square, The Crossroads of the World, as some called that expensive piece of real estate, is a showcase of modernity and vice. Mark missed its alluring sights as he rode under it in a noisy subway, heading uptown. Upon debarking, he studied the diagram and location of the Columbia University campus, which he had received in the mail. After getting his directions, he ignored the beehive of yellow cabs prowling the streets for business and set out on foot. He looked for the building circled in red on his map where he would lodge for two days.

Mark had done his research on education well. As he entered the famous campus, he reminded himself of the crucial role the place played in the history of education in America. The secular humanist forces reshaped education there, inciting the cultural war that spread throughout American schools. It had started at the beginning of the last century. And here he was, a country bumpkin bringing back to this center of culture a portion of his young mind—a sharp mind shaped by this place's long arms and dexterous hands. Mark felt himself strongly motivated, eager to go. Honesdale, Pennsylvania seemed far away, and Abby—a pretty flower left by the road to wither. He tugged at the rings of his armor, bravely trying to close the gap opened in it last Christmas, after being weakened on Nine-eleven. He felt he was not succeeding very well.

But his speech did go well that evening. Professor Shorham was there. And so were a couple of other teachers from Philadelphia who knew the bright former editor of the school paper. Donna came to him, too, joining the chorus of accolades. She was quick to remind Mark of her promise to be his valentine for a day. The feminine cruelty had melted. She knew a winner when she saw one.

Following Mark's talk, the four hundred conventioneers went back to their various study groups into which they had been distributed since morning. Under the tutelage of well-known experts on various political issues, young minds were being furnished with the latest weapons with which to take their place in the cultural war. The convention organizers looked at the students as soldiers to divide into corps. There were sessions on feminism; gay, women and minority rights; environment; ecology and other cultural issues to be fashioned into war material. A secondary teachers' group had been formed to learn how to teach their students to be sympathetic with the activists when they began to fight again. The conventioneers should be prepared for action as soon as the truce was broken. This was to take place after America invaded Iraq as expected. The respite brought about by the wave of patriotism that engulfed the nation since Nine-eleven was not expected to last. It would start dwindling down with the vision of blood and body bags in full color splashed on every TV screen in the nation.

Not appointed to any group, since he had come in late, Mark had to choose a study group for himself. Enthusiastic in the role of education in his Ideological World, he picked the teachers group. The session was lead by a professor who taught at the university hosting the convention. Dr. Pacetta was an emaciated woman of indefinable age with expertise in the tenets of evolution. She boasted a smattering of psychology behind her illustrious academic career. Mark guessed that was why she was chosen to head the session. In her presentation and in her answers to questions it was evident that she thought of education and evolution as intrinsically linked together. She pointed out that as mankind evolves biologically toward physical perfection, proper education produces the material for the mental evolution of the species. It is with that in mind that teachers should teach, she said. Students were to be taught to admire political activists. All the antiquated values and morés that hold back societal and human biological evolution must be trashed if the future was to be better than the present. Since all issues were political issues, progressive political activists in the field of education played a key role in the evolutionary process of man.

Mark didn't ask any question or offer any comment. All the time he spent in the session he was trying to chase away the picture of a flower that he thought had been left to wither by the side of the evolutionary road. The flower of his metaphor was intelligent, bright. How was it that this unique individual with her distinctive values and beliefs was a hindrance to mankind's evolution? Even as he pondered the answer, he instinctively pulled up his armor tighter. He felt that intellectual honesty demanded this measure.

By ten o'clock Mark was left alone with his thoughts.

His time in the spotlight was short and now gone. Everybody scrambled after the study sessions were over, each individual seeking his own way of spending what was left of the evening. At the entrance to the hall of the convention building, he spied Donna laughing and talking in one of the telephone booths. He and Donna had made no appointment to meet after the sessions. Mark felt he was not ready for her. His mind was feverish. His thoughts were consequential, disturbing, and he could not pin them down. He was going to need time to sort them out, and to do this he needed to be alone. He decided to claim his own right to exercise his own form of masculine cruelty and avoid Donna. Mark lengthened his steps and left the building.

Outside, a young man approached Mark, boldly. His first words gave him away. "Hey, man! That was quite a speech you made this evening. The program says that you haven't graduated yet in journalism. Is it right?"

"That's right. I still have a few months of cramming to go. Why do you ask?" Mark kept his voice smooth and cool in trying to conceal his impatience at the young man's greeting.

"You sounded so sure of your subject matter that I thought they were pulling a fast one on us." The young man laughed. "You sounded as if you were already writing for the New York Times."

Mark didn't know how to respond to this. He had detected a note of cynicism.

"Anyway," the intruder proceeded, giving no importance to what he had just said, "you staying in a sorority for the night?"

"No, I am staying in the campus guest house." Mark didn't want to be rude and excuse himself, although he was tempted. What was the fellow after? Why didn't he leave?

"I've never been there. Are there girls there? I'd be surprised if not. Dames and weeds are aplenty everywhere."

Mark was about to walk out on the inquirer; then

changed his mind. He wanted to know more. The fellow pricked his curiosity.

"Are you a student here, Mr.—?"

"Matt Bacardi. Skip the Mister. I guess you can say I am a student here. I take a few courses here and there, just to keep the old folks happy."

"If you are not that much interested in an education, why did you come to a convention like this? This is serious business. We don't have time to chase after girls and certainly have no interest in drugs. We are interested in finding what's best for our country."

Matt laughed. "Where have you been all these years, Targett?" he sneered. "Bet you are from the sticks. Half of the people here don't give a hoot about the things you are saying. What people are interested in is in what takes place at night, not during the meetings. Everybody knows that."

"Is that so?" Mark replied. "Aren't you being too cynical about this?"

"You can't be a cynic when you are telling the truth. As for you, you are as naive as they come. This whole convention is a gag. They spent a fortune putting it together just as a tribute to themselves. They don't even use their own money. The dough comes from lefties and downright commies. I never bought this country-and-doing-what's-best-for-it-business even before I got the dope of what really goes on behind the curtain. All right, call me cynical if you want to, but I am really just the kind of guy that likes to tell it like it is. Sorry I interrupted your daydreaming. I didn't intend to. I was just trying to be neighborly when I recognized you. And I wanted to let you know that I thought you are a good speechwriter. You'll be a good journalist yet, I am sure, but you surely need to come to grips with reality before what you write will do any good. Have a good evening. I hope you have enough conventioneers tomorrow still able to keep their eyes open after all that will be going on tonight." After his long and blunt speech, Matt Bacardi walked away, leaving a speech-less Mark Targett standing there.

Mark saw Donna leave the building, but she didn't see him. He made no move to go after her. He was angry, bewil-dered, and ashamed all at the same time. Was this young man right? He thoughtfully watched some of the people thronging the sidewalks. What were they there for? Taking his troubled thoughts with him to bed, he tossed and turned restlessly.

When he returned to the conference room next morning the first thing he noticed was how tired and sleepy-eyed the students looked. Had Matt been right? They were tripping over one another reaching for the coffee pot that was always available in the foyer.

Mark revolved Matt's unrequested report on the falseness of his fellows on campus. His mind raced toward a conclu-sion. By linking biological and mental evolution, Pacetta raised in Mark's mind a thought he had never come across in all the years he studied the postulates of the theory of evolu-tion. The cynical young man had given him the needed pin to fasten the illusive thought to solid ground. And it was so simple that Mark wondered how he missed it before.

Dr. Pacetta had made it clear that evolutionists expected the biological betterment of humankind to be accomplished through an evolutionary process couched on the survival of the fittest. Procreation was the engine of that process. Accelerate the engine and quicken the progress. The promo-tion of 'free love' could be based on this premise. That means that the intense procreative activities going on all last night, according to Matt Bacardi, could be deemed a good thing, in line with the progressive situation-ethics code. Of course, the bluff was called on evolution's helping hands after the morn-ing-after pill was swallowed with the morning coffee. The solution then to cooperate effectively with nature's evolution-ary process had to be selective mating. That could well explain the abortionists' desire to ensure that every child was a 'wanted child.' However, Hitler had tried that selective technique before, with disastrous consequences.

And then the probability that a 20th century man was walking on the moon on the same day that a cannibal in the jungle ate his enemy didn't speak well for Dr. Pacetta's theory. Her linking biological to mental perfection by education might be a good PR for evolution. But, in all actuality, given the same educational opportunities, what could the primitive jungle man do in his lifetime? What if he mastered a civilized language and gained up-to-date expertise, cultivated his culture and values, and became in his lifetime the superman divined for him by evolutionists for thousands of years from now? Mark didn't know where this thought would lead him, but he knew he had already retrieved the pretty flower from the side of the road where he had impulsively left it the previous day.

All that day he divided his attention between the speakers at the podium and the nonstop speaker within his mind. First, he concluded that Matt Bacardi was right. Mark was naive. He knew what the humanistic beliefs were doing to people, especially young people. Sexual freedom had transformed the most tender relationship to a costly ride in a carousel of instant pleasure and self-gratification. The enslaving sexual freedom came packaged with the approval of peers and preachers of secular humanism. Mark had generously turned a blind eye to what was happening around him on the campus. He knew he could no longer do that. If things in this city were as bad as he was finding them to be, he could foresee the failure of his ideological mission of changing this country and the world. In reality, moral looseness would continue to enlarge the already existing breach between east and west. Had history chosen New York City for her human drama as the stage where the western culture was to live or die?

Mark came across Donna several times during the morning. They talked briefly as they crossed paths. And they had lunch together in the cafeteria. There they talked about their common past experiences. Donna couldn't help but talk about her future. She was excited about it. She was going to go a long way with upward moving politicians. Why should Mark be stuck in a hack job in a hick town after his graduation when he could be with her in Washington and move up? And she hadn't been given the opportunity to keep her promise about being his valentine. "I don't know where you disappeared to last night," she giggled slyly. "You had better not do the same today."

But he didn't listen to her. Two hours after they lunched together Mark was on his way to the bus station to take the three o'clock bus back to Honesdale. Through a mutual acquaintance, he sent Donna a note written on his sales representative card: *"Sorry, Valentine, I must be home before dark. Good luck with your Washington job. Mark."* The note was curt, but he felt that as a feminist she could handle it. Mark had lost respect for her.

Before leaving the guest building, he looked over the tourist card rack by the checkout counter. He picked one with a picture of a New York skyscraper. The Twin Towers still graced the photo. While writing Abby's name and address on it, he wondered if the card would become valuable as an antique someday. He thoughtfully chewed the tip of his pen; then wrote, *"Thank you for your card. All's well, but someone called me a hick here. I'm about to leave the wicked city for our hick town. See you by our pumpkin patch. Mark."* He bought a stamp in the coin machine, attaching it to the card before dropping it in the mailbox. He picked up his valise and attaché case and walked out into the chilly afternoon.

CHAPTER 19

"Two Peas in a Pod"

The winter seemed reluctant to leave northeastern Pennsylvania. Mark pulled out of Main Street onto route 670 on a Monday late afternoon wondering whether winter was going to blast the area with more snow before leaving. He would be at the Swingle's in the next few minutes. What would it be like to have dinner with Abby and her mother? He had been looking forward to this since last Thursday, when he had gotten the invitation. Would he feel like a fish out of water in their company? Or, worse, like a fish in a bowl? All the association he had lately had been with female company. Should he attach any meaning to that?

The previous Thursday when Abby and her mother had come in to the store, he had immediately thought, "Two peas in a pod!" It was his first time to meet Abby's mother. Looking at Martha Swingle closer he realized that her features were unlike Abby's in many ways. Her face was bright like Abby's and graced with that same perennial smile people at peace with themselves and the world exhibit. But the skin was darker and the eyes were not round and green as Abby's were. Her hair, black as the hair of the other pea, was precociously gray at the temples, with no trace of having been ever disguised with tint. Like Abby, she was not ugly yet not much of a beauty either. Her features were harmonious and pleasant. As it sometimes happens at first meetings, she reminded Mark of somebody he had seen before, but could not remember who or where.

"Hi Mark!" Abby had greeted him with that mischievous smile she always wore. "This is my Mom. She is Martha and she already knows all that I know about you, which isn't much. We two decided that we ought to change that by having you come for dinner Monday evening. I know you are off work then; so what's your excuse?" She managed all this without stopping for breath or dropping the smile. Mark's responding smile turned into laughter as Abby went along nonstop. As it happened every time she behaved and spoke that way, he found himself floundering without his pet phrases.

Martha came to his rescue. "Mark, please don't mind this impetuous daughter of mine. She doesn't seem to realize that not everybody has had nineteen years of training in putting up with her as I have. By the way, glad to make your acquaintance, Mark."

And that was how things went that blustery Thursday morning. They agreed on the time of the dinner. Abby drew a map of the way to their house on a pad she found on the counter. Then they started to leave, as quickly as they had come, but not before Abby warned, shaking a threatening finger, "You'd better be careful, Mark. You are coming to enemy's territory. But don't worry; we don't shoot daggers at anybody." She paused, before pleasantly but seriously adding, "We just poison them."

Mark never looked at the map Abby had drawn until he drove past the small park in 'downtown' Bethany. Mark had loved the village ever since he had found it years ago when the Targetts had moved from upstate New York to northeastern Pennsylvania. Now he looked at the drawing. "*Turn right here.*" Abby had underlined *here*. The *here* was Church Street. "*Third house on your right,*" was the instruction given after the here. He turned obediently into a driveway with a slight decline. The house was small and cheerful, with plenty of trees, now bare. He pictured them all dressed in green and, later, in yellows and browns. The Swingle's place would be even more cheerful in the months to come, he speculated. He was sure there would be plenty of flowers all around to add color to the scenery.

Mark parked the car in front of the basement garage. He heard a sound above his head and looked up to see a window sash going up and a happy voice calling, "Mark! Use the front door." Abby pointed in the direction. "Burt is at attention at the back door and he loves company too much." She started to shut the window, then, as an afterthought, added, "Burt is the dog, not the butler!"

Laughing, Mark walked around the side of the pleasant looking house and stepped up to the front door. Martha Swingle opened the door for him.

"Welcome, Mark." Martha said. " No, don't worry about your shoes. Here, let me take your coat." There was no stiffness or awkwardness. He heard the pleading bark of Burt in the back hall. Abby was already juggling pans in the kitchen.

"Hi Mark!" Abby called. "Be right with you. As soon as I finish with the arsenic." Martha and Mark laughed together as Mark glanced around the homey room.

"What a clown!" Martha Swingle laughed.

It was a good start. After freeing himself of his heavy winter jacket, Mark stepped into the small dining room/living room surrounding the kitchen. He was already feeling at home, though the decor of the house was unmistakably feminine. After he sat on the florid couch, Abby came out of the kitchen wiping her hands on her red apron. Mark got up to meet her. She shook Mark's hand. That was the second time she had done that. He was surprised. Young people just didn't shake hands anymore.

"You'd better be hungry, young man," she quipped, "We'll have baked lasagna for dinner. Mother and I love it. We'd rather eat lasagna than be slender and famished. I hope you like pasta. I forgot to ask you before what you like to eat and whether you are on a diet, though you don't look as if you need one."

"Lasagna happens to be my favorite dish, Abby. Did your guardian angel tell you that?"

"No. I haven't seen him in a while. I have been very naughty lately and he's been staying away. I could tell you that a bird told me, but I know I couldn't fool you. Birds are not back in town yet. There's no mystery to it. We are just being selfish, that's all."

While Mark and Abby talked, Martha came out of the kitchen carrying a steaming baked casserole to the table.

"You young'uns stop talking and come to the table. If you need to wash your hands, Mark, the bathroom is over there," she pointed with her nose, "Left of the front door." Abby clarified Martha's directions by showing Mark where the bathroom was. When he returned to the dining room, the two girls were standing one on each side of the table. Mark found that they were going to have him sit at the head of the table. He was about to pull the chair out for the older woman when both girls sat down themselves. Mark sat down, too, a little uncomfortable. They would say grace before eating. His place at the head of the table might be a silent request for him to do the honor. There was a moment of awkward silence.

Abby broke the silence. "Mother and I agreed a long time ago that whoever cooked the meal leads in prayer at mealtime. I've done all the cooking today; so here we go." And without any more ado, she said grace. She prayed extemporaneously and talked with God as if she were talking with the person nearest to her, which was Mark. She gave thanks for the food and for having Mark with them.

After her Amen, Mark asked, "Which of you ends up saying grace more often?" The girls didn't seem to detect the bit of suspicion in the question. Could Abby be lying to make him comfortable?

"Mother does," Abby answered him promptly. "Mother is the official homemaker. I work and study. Mother just teaches school a few hours a day."

"Abby, dear, are you implying that homemaking is not work?" Mark caught a glimmer of the same disarming trait of mischievousness in Martha that he had learned to expect in Abby.

"Oh, oh, looks like I said the wrong thing. Help me, Mark!"

Mark couldn't be of any help. All he could do was enjoy the company of two down-to-earth ladies who seemed to take pleasure in life and in each other. How generous they were, to share that satisfaction with him by encircling him within their pleasantness. He hadn't experienced that sense of well-being since his grandfather had died. The senior Targett had enjoyed life. And he had shared that joy with his little namesake every time he was with him. Could it be the girls' relationship to God that made him joyful at their table? And where had Papa's joy come from? He remembered Papa talking about God to him, but little Mark had been too young to understand. Everybody talked about God in those days. Even his father who abandoned them, and his mother whose smiles and words he had never been able to trust. And his older sister who had been unkind to him whenever she did happen to notice him. Grandmother, too. In the past, Granny had mentioned God only in passing, as if He existed only by her invitation, at her choice of time and location.

"Have we lost you, Mark?" Martha's voice interrupted his thoughts. Both had noticed Mark eating absentmindedly.

"No, I am right here, Mrs. Swingle," then, remembering Abby's question, "You don't need my help. As a matter of fact, I don't think you really want it. I am the one who needs help in thinking and saying the right thing. We often mean more than our words say, and say more than we intend to mean. My grandmother just told me the other day that she is waiting for me to finish chasing dragons before she presents me with something of the past that can be helpful in my future. It is a colorful expression. I have no idea where she found it. But I knew precisely what she meant when I heard her say it. You are good with words, Abby. Do you know what the phrase means?"

"I think I might know what it means," Abby answered, remembering what she had learned about Mark by studying his carefully written speech outline. There was much to say to him about chasing dragons. She knew she had been hiding the seriousness of her concern for Mark by sounding frivolous, but he ought to know and she ought to tell him what she knew. "Oh! Jesus, dear Jesus," she prayed silently, "I need wisdom beyond my years."

CHAPTER 20

Looking Left

❧

"Have we lost you, Abby?" Mark mimicked Martha. Abby hadn't realized she had stopped eating.

Martha knew what was in Abby's mind and the reason for the direction the conversation was taking. She had read Mark's speech outline with Abby. She knew the depth of his involvement with the dragons of the world. She also knew her daughter's mind as well as anybody could know a child's mind. It was not difficult for her to understand what the two youths were facing. Mark seemed unsure about the things he had learned, and was apparently humble enough to hint that. And she understood well the kind of person her daughter was. Abby was intensely sensitive to people's needs and was willing to give much. But she was still too young to know when to give and how much to give. Being able to comprehend all this, Martha must find out what should be her own part in the youthful conflict. Did Abby know her role?

Abby broke the silence. "You were about to," she confessed. "Thanks for bringing me back. I was thinking about your speech. I am afraid that my comments could easily make you distance yourself."

"If I promise to stand by you no matter what, would you tell me what you'd say about my speech?"

"I thank you for the encouragement, Mark. I need it, for I fear I ought to say what is on my mind no matter whether you stand by me or start after another dragon. I have no choice."

"I am all ears, Abby."

Martha got up and started clearing the table. "You two keep talking. We'll have our dessert later on. You drink coffee, Mark? Abby does."

"Yes, please, but not too strong," Mark answered before turning his full attention to Abby.

"Mark, you have not been looking in both directions before crossing streets that must be crossed. You can get hurt that way. I fault your schooling for this. You have been taught to look to your left only, as if the world has only one-way streets. This book—" pointing to the Bible on the stand behind her, "—is the only available source of factual information about the dangers of the two-way traffic pattern of human reality. No one is prepared to live or die without the truths this manual for living teaches. Yet modern education has done away with it." Abby was silent for a moment.

"Is your two-way street analogy political or philosophical?" Mark wondered.

"You divorce politics from sound thinking at your own risk." Abby replied feelingly. "Whoever coined the phrase 'ignorance is bliss' was describing what I call the Irrational Age of our muddled culture."

Mark was silent for a moment, digesting the thoughts presented to him. Then he asked, "When you say that I have only been looking to my left before crossing a street do you mean to imply that the right is where God is? You know by now that I am an agnostic. If the right side of the street is where God is I can't possibly blame my schooling. God is not in its curricula. And that is as it should be."

Abby looked distressed. "Mark, I cannot blame you for not believing in God. Your concept of God, and that of those who educated you, makes Him a very small entity—a god you create in your own image. That god, of course does not exist, except as a thought in your finite mind. From a human point of view, you should be commended for your intellectual honesty."

Mark had to admit that this thought was new to him. "What size is your God, Abby?" Mark asked, adroitly.

"If I knew a quantitative answer to this question my god would be as small as yours. A famous logician of the last century whose works I am familiar with would answer your question this way: 'the universe is composed of billions of worlds whirling in a space whose measure is beyond our comprehension.' But our Creator didn't leave us in darkness here. With the measurement instrument of logic He gave us, we can conclude that a Creator must be above His creation in grandeur and power. It is illogical to think of God as being within the space He created—space, immeasurable as it is, is within God. Our minds alone cannot fathom such immensity as our ears and eyes are limited to fixed frequencies. To doubt God's existence or to predicate God as non-existent is to rattle our prison chains. The Uncreated Light that is God, His infinitude, can only be perceived through the eyes of faith. I am perfectly content in not knowing in human terms the full extent of my God's size, but I know that my security, my life, my eternal destiny are in better hands than in that of any power we are able to measure."

Again, Mark had to acknowledge having never thought of God that way. Did Dr. Pacetta ever think of God that way?

"If that is your view of God, Abby, why did I just hear you address Him as if He were sitting across the table from you?"

"Oh! Mark, don't you see? I addressed God as if He was sitting across the table from me because He was sitting across the table from me. And you should know why we couldn't see Him. If we could see Him He would be your god, not my God. And, Mark, I have no need of a god like that and you don't either. Your speech precluded the existence of your god, not mine. My God was looking over your shoulder as you wrote your speech, whether you ever knew it or not. He is present everywhere as the Holy Spirit except in the human heart that refuses Him. He honors the dignity of choice. We call that free will. That is the real source of human freedom about which we so glibly speak. Your humanism tramples this badge of human dignity while claiming to honor it. You want a better America, a better world. Your speech makes that clear. And that is good. But so did Hitler and Stalin, who, like you, denied a Creator God. Countless millions lost their freedom and died undignified deaths because of it. There are no Gulags or death camps in America yet, but over forty million babies have already been sacrificed before the altar of the god of hedonism your secular humanism created to replace God the Creator." The tears flowed down Abby's cheeks as she looked at Mark.

Mark's thoughts reviewed not only his beliefs, but also his very life. He knew what was happening on college and university campuses and even in high schools where God was denied. The excesses and the drunkenness, the lack of restraint, the I-can-do-anything-I-want-to-do attitude. He had tried for years not to make too much of it. He had been taught that the morés of the past were in the way of human evolution to perfect good. And he had believed it. Was it because of the absence of those morés that his generation was experiencing such tragic results? Mark had tried to convince himself that the wantonness, the sexual promiscuity, drugs, crimes, abortions, and the wave of teenagers' suicide would be a temporary thing—the side effect of the powerful medicine to cure humanity's ills that humanism had prescribed and the western civilization was religiously taking. Mark himself had remained a moral person. He was too busy in the vanguard of his crusaders for a better America, for a better world, to allow instinctive forces to be out of his control. It is true that other political movements under naturalism had failed. Recent history attested to that. But with America, it should be different; he felt there was a chance to succeed. America had all the elements to succeed where others had failed. That was how he understood the uniqueness of a nation nobody seemed properly able to define. Marco Nemo called it "the most fitting habitat for humankind to live and thrive." That was what made the nation rich and powerful. Wasn't that what he was trying to share with the world and with the downtrodden in America?

All the while, Mark was reviewing his beliefs and goals, both youth were silent. It was not an awkward silence. It was like the calming of the waves after a storm. During that silent interlude, Abby reached for her Bible.

Mark watched the girl to find what she would do. Abby opened the book and extracted from it a typewritten paper. It was Mark's speech outline. She spread the sheets over the table, and ran her hand over them to smooth the creases. She was pensive and anxious. But, noticing his curious look, she quipped, "Don't worry, Mark. I am not going to preach to you. But I need you to know," she continued, "that I have spent more time with this outline of your creed since you shared it with me than with my lessons in biology. Not only have I spent time studying your ideas in the light of the Scriptures, I have invested much time interceding to God in your behalf. I seek no credit for doing this and I don't feel I am any better than you are for doing it. I am constrained to bring your attention to the other direction you were taught not to bother with before you cross another street. Because you don't see God, you don't believe in Him. Has it ever occurred to you, Mark, that God has actually sat across the table from men and women in time and history before dying as a man dies, then rising from death to be seen no more except through the eyes of faith?"

Abby picked up the Bible again and continued, "That's what this Book is all about. I could trace for you from Genesis to Revelation the whole story of God revealing Himself to mankind. But you are not quite prepared to be told that. To receive it and find meaning for your life from birth to death and all that is in between and beyond requires intelligent faith. You have enough intelligence, but your faith is nonexistent yet. That's why I have been praying for you every day since I told you that my name came from the Bible," and here she broke into a smile, "and you said 'oh!' …And here comes Mother with my coconut pie. Do you want a scoop of ice cream on top of your piece? I wish we could put as much faith in your heart as the pounds of fat we are putting on your waist tonight. But we cannot. Only God can do that."

Mark sensed the intensity of Abby's final remarks, although she had lightly veiled it with a smile.

CHAPTER 21

Music in the Chapel

The nursing home where Helen worked as Activities Director was located between Honesdale and Bethany. It was a rich-looking set of buildings designed to give an atmosphere of refinement. The well-kept gardens and richly decorated interiors spoke of beauty and opulence. From the road that passed by, it was hidden. Mark contemplated the grounds as he parked his car a little distance from the main entrance.

He was visiting the Pocono Nursing Home to see his mother. Mark had wanted to know how Grandmother Targett's plans to sell her house and move in with her daughter were coming along. He couldn't get hold of either of the women, even though he had left messages on their answering machines twice. This Sunday morning he called the home and asked for the Activities Director. They were having some difficulty in finding her; so Mark decided he would just drive the six or seven miles to the place and see his mother in person. The sun was shining brightly and the temperature rose as a prelude to the coming spring.

At the entrance desk, the receptionist promptly dialed Helen's number. But the Activity Director was not in her office. The Pocono Home was a large place.

"I will page her, sir," she told Mark. "Why don't you have a seat in the visitor's lounge while I locate her? Who shall I say you are?"

"Mark. Mark Targett. I am her son."

The visitor's lounge, like the rest of the place, was richly decorated. There were plenty of pictures on the walls, all done in pastel colors. Rather than sit down on one of the inviting sofas, Mark studied the pictures while waiting for his mother. They were landscape scenes of the sort that is supposed to induce the viewer into a sense of peace and tranquility. They were generally large, except one next to an aquarium where various kinds of colorful fish swam languidly. Mark went to inspect the smaller picture. It was a plaque with a poem written clearly, in large letters, and surrounded at the right side and bottom with bright wild flowers. It was artistically done. The golden, elaborate eight-by-ten frame and matting enhanced the richness of the picture. Mark relished all that before reading the poem. It was entitled "Old Age's Joy."

> *Pity me not, my fair young friend*
> *Because I'm old*
> *And hurt hurts more, steep is so steep*
> *And cold so cold.*
> *For there's a spring of joy my age*
> *Hides within me,*
> *About to swell and flow throughout*
> *Eternity.*
> *Old folks know best how hope grows brighter*
> *Day by day,*
> *When time and pain were joined by faith*
> *Along the way.*

The faith which knows that God Himself
Suffered as Man
And with His death purchased my life,
Then rose again.

So never, never think of me
Out of context.
Already Christ redeemed my soul.
My body is next!

As he neared the end of the piece, the meaning started to escape him, though the flowing rhythm still delighted his poetical taste. The idea of faith acknowledging that God became a man brought Abby to mind. She had mentioned something at her table about a revelation of God in the presence of faith. That recollection put the possible meaning of the poem back on track. But the last four lines threw him off again. Then his eyes turned to the name of the poet in small print at the bottom. It read—Marco Nemo.

Mark was still staring at the picture with amazement when he heard his mother's voice behind him, "Mark! What a delightful surprise!"

Did she sound as if she really meant it or was he loosing his sense of factuality.

"I've been trying to contact you since yesterday. Granny didn't answer the phone either and your people here don't ever know where you are. So I decided to drive over. I needed to know if there's any development in Granny's plans. Is there any problem with her? Is that why she doesn't answer the phone?"

"Sorry, Mark. I should have let you know. My mother is here in the home with me until my car is fixed. It conked out on me again. I was worried about not being able to go to her; so I brought her to stay here in our guest room for a couple of days until I have the car back. We do have some people looking into buying Mother's house. How did it go with your speaking engagement in New York?"

"OK I guess." Mark didn't want to talk about it. Not with his mother. "I came back the next day. I don't care much for big cities." Then, turning to the wall, "Mother, how did that picture get here?"

"That? Mr. Nemo, the author, presented the framed poem to the home. He does the artwork you see in that picture too. They're florals he constructs with pressed flowers. That's his hobby. We all know him here. He and Mrs. Nemo come here often to entertain our guests. Actually the Nemos are holding the morning service here today at ten o'clock. They are covering for the home's chaplain who is out of town today. Why don't you stay for their program?"

"The Nemos read poems to the residents?"

"No. They present musical programs. Their music is very much appreciated by our old folks. The Nemos real ministry is among Alzheimer patients. Mrs. Nemo plays the harp, accompanied by her husband on the piano. Dementia patients respond very well to their program of therapeutic music."

"I have read of the latest medical findings on the effects of certain music on people with that kind of illness. Is their fee high?"

"They don't charge anything. Do stay. Mother will be in the audience and I am sure she'd love to see you. You'll enjoy the Nemos too."

Mark was tempted. He was curious to know what else there was to learn about the mysterious old man of his Nine-eleven experience. He looked at his watch. It was 9:30.

"OK mother. I'll stay. Is there a place here where the son of the Activity Director can have a cup of coffee? It's that time again for me."

A few minutes before 10:00 Mark was with Grace Targett in the home's cozy chapel. His grandmother insisted on sitting up front. Mark didn't want to be recognized, so he excused himself and sat further back.

His mother was already coordinating the program with the Nemos. A beautiful, full-size harp had already been placed by the baby grand piano. Most of the white haired audience had been waiting for nearly twenty minutes, but a few of the guests were still being wheeled into the chapel.

The Nemos were sitting near their instruments. This was the first time Mark had seen Mrs. Nemo up close. Her hair was white, like her husband's, but she had European features and color that contrasted with her husband's darker skin. She seemed to be the same height as Mr. Nemo. She was dressed in a flowery Swiss dress with a long skirt. Over it was a Swiss apron.

Mark's mother introduced them to the audience in case some of the residents were seeing them for the first time. Marco Nemo motioned for his wife to introduce their program. Mrs. Nemo did so. She was gracious and humble as she told the residents, mostly ladies, to feel free to sing softly along with the songs they recognized.

As an afterthought, Mr. Nemo joined his wife in the presentation. "Do, join us in singing," he invited. "In our playing we concentrate on the words. They are more important than the music. Our music is only the carrier of the message of the song. Let the words sink into your minds and hearts. They express truths by which we can live and die. You might hear me singing them softly myself. But don't follow me. I'll probably be singing in my own language."

The audience laughed at this.

When they finished speaking, instead of going to her harp Mrs. Nemo sat at the piano. The piano sat at an angle so the people could see her hands. For a moment, she seemed to be praying. Every one was silent, their eyes fixed on her. Mrs. Nemo moved her hand slowly above the piano keys; then brought them down, softly. The place seemed filled with the sound of church bells. It was like a call for the faithful to come in and worship. The harmonious sounds moved into a crescendo, staying loud for a few seconds before descending, softly, unhurriedly, into a musical whisper as church bells do. There was a silent emotion in the air. You could hardly notice when the bell sounds turned into the captivating melody of "The Church in the Wildwood." A few in the audience recognized the song and joined in soft singing, as if to themselves:

> There's a church in the valley by the wildwood,
> No lovelier spot in the dale;
> No place is so dear to my childhood
> As the little brown church in the vale.

By the time the piano started to play the chorus half the audience had joined in:

> Oh, come, come, come, come!
> Come to the church in the wildwood,
> Oh, come to the church in the vale.
> No spot is so dear to my childhood
> As the little brown church in the vale.

The pianist changed smoothly from one song to another, playing old hymns well known by a good number of people in the audience. No announcements were made in between the numbers. There was nothing to interrupt the flow of the music. Mrs. Nemo's playing style made the piano sound almost like a harp. She used no artifice and exhibited no technique. It was pure, simple melody playing, accentuating the words of the song, with tastefully embellishing chords and frills. Many joined in as soon as they recognized each new song.

Half an hour went by without Mark sensing the passing

of time. The musician brought the last song to a resting note
at both top and bottom of the keyboard, stood up quietly,
and seated herself behind the harp. Marco Nemo went to the
piano. Mrs. Nemo leaned her harp on her right shoulder and
glided her old hands over the strings in evocative runs.
There is no instrument more able to move souls as the runs
of a softly played harp. At the piano, Mr. Nemo gently
played the chords his wife strummed. There was harmony
and beauty coming out of the two pairs of hands. Some in
the audience wept. At nearly eleven o'clock, the pianist cut
into the undertone with which the two instruments held the
hearers in a trance. A loud staccato like a trumpet preceded
a powerful baritone voice that betrayed the singer's age:

> God of our fathers, whose almighty hand
> Leads forth in beauty all the starry band
> Of shining worlds in splendor thro' the skies,
> Our grateful songs before Thy throne arise.

> Thy love divine hath led us in the past,
> In this free land by Thee our lot is cast;
> Be Thou our Ruler, Guardian, Guide and Stay,
> Thy word our law, Thy paths our chosen way.

> From war's alarms, from deadly pestilence,
> Be Thy strong arm our ever strong defense;
> Thy true religion in our hearts increase,
> Thy bounteous goodness nourish us in peace.

> Refresh Thy people on their toilsome way,
> Lead us from night to never-ending day;
> Fill all our lives with love and grace divine,
> And glory, laud and praise be ever Thine.

Every word of the enduring national song was clear.

There was no sign of a foreign accent in the soloist's voice.

Silence followed the song. No one stirred. Mr. Nemo walked to the lectern. With the arpeggios of the harp for background, the old man recited feelingly, in his powerful voice: "Now unto Him who is able to keep you from falling, and to present you faultless before the presence of His glory with exceeding joy, to the only wise God our Savior, be glory and majesty, dominion and power, both now and ever. Amen."

This time Mark detected his accent, and recognized it as the same as when the old man had spoken of his America.

The Nemos sat down again without any further word. The place was so quiet that the heating system fan could be heard. Nobody stirred. People didn't seem to want to leave the place.

In the silence, Mark's thoughts roamed between Bethany and the Catskills where he had grown up. He could see with his mind's eye the little churches dotting the countryside. It seemed these old folks could see the end of their lives approaching; yet they looked at death with a song on their lips—faith, God, and country. For him it was country and world. What was faith? Was it Nemo's poem and Abby's emotional words before the coconut pie dessert? Papa must have had faith too. He died with a smile on his lips. Mark saw it himself when he was taken into the room where Papa laid dead. Mark had been stunned by grief. He could not cry even then. A voice had assured him, "Don't cry, Marky, your Papa is in heaven now and he is happy." He hadn't even looked to see who it was that said it. The scene with all its deep meaning had been purposely buried somewhere deep inside by Mark himself. In the same dark crevice he had also tried to bury the God who had taken his Papa away from him. Teachers and textbooks had covered the hollow it had made in his heart and he had grown up to be Mark Targett, the skeptic.

A stir within the room broke the spell. Helen's voice was subdued and sincere as she thanked the people for coming and the Nemos for sharing their talents.

Before leaving the building, Mark stopped at the visitor's lounge and read Nemo's poem again. He reached for the small pad he always carried with him in his jacket to jot down his thoughts and quickly wrote the "The Old Age's Joy" down. He ought to find out about the substance the word faith tried to represent. When Mark walked out into the sunshine, he wished he didn't have to be with people at the store today.

CHAPTER 22

My Body is Next

M arch came determined to hold its ground. It melted most of the snow, got the temperature above fifty, and coaxed some grass to show what she could of her green. Even the robins mistook the warm winter sunshine for springtime. Here and there in back yards, they were pushing aside what they thought was the last of the snow to dig out unwary worms.

The day Mark took Grandmother Targett for a ride in his sports car was one of those sunny March days. When Grace asked her grandson to take her out in the countryside, she had an ulterior motive. She needed to talk to Mark before he left for Philadelphia. And she wanted to visit his grandfather's grave with him. The Targetts had originally been from the area before straying north into New York State. The old family burial plot had been waiting all those years to receive the next dead.

Mark was about to leave for his final stretch at the university. The Santilli's had gotten back from their winter sojourn in Florida near the end of February. They already had another renter ready to take Mark's place as soon as he vacated the apartment. With all these moving arrangements, he had not seen Abby much. He missed the girl and wished he could spend some time with her before leaving.

Granny had sold her house with most of her furniture. With the help of David, one of his few friends, and a rented U-Haul truck, Mark moved the rest of her belongings to her daughter's house. Grace Targett, seeing her past dissolving in the disappearing items, had cried silently. But she was a brave soul. She knew she was nearing the end of her earthly journey, and she accepted the fact stoically. She was not in pain, at least not yet, but the doctor didn't promise an easy end. When Mark picked her up after Sunday dinner and helped her into his car, he found her much feebler than when he had last seen her.

The Canaan cemetery occupied just about three acres of land on the south of the hamlet. A narrow country road separated it from another graveyard that was part of a Russian monastery and church. Not even the commonality of death can keep people from being divided. The Targetts plot was at the south side of the burial ground. There were no enclosures on the side of the cemetery where the road bent sharply in the direction of Honesdale. An old stone wall encircled the other three sides. There were plenty of trees around, getting ready to welcome the spring. As Mark pulled his car to the side of the road, he couldn't help contrasting his Granny with the trees. To the trees the coming spring was to bring a new surge of life, and to Granny, Mark was sure, death. The last lines of Nemo's poem came to mind then:

> So never, never think of me
> Out of context.
> Already Christ redeemed my soul.
> My body is next.

Mark understood intellectually what Nemo was trying

to say with those lines, but, as he reminded himself, words were deceiving. A good poet might do an excellent job of conveying emotions through poetry, but how about truth? Even the reality of human life would be wiped out before the eyes to be renamed dust, worms, and bones. How was one to guess where the card of truth would be after reality shuffled the deck?

Mark noted that the snow, which had been almost a constant companion throughout the winter, had melted away. Most graves were in need of a good spring-cleaning. The living should soon be picking up the debris of winter lying around the places of the dead.

Mark fought the tentacles of sadness as he approached Papa's tombstone. Youth and age stood silently before Grandfather's grave. How frail Granny looked standing there in the soft breeze! She shivered though the temperature was close to sixty. Mark could almost hear Nemo's words as if coming from her:

> Pity me not, my fair young friend,
> Because I'm old
> And hurt hurts more, steep is so steep
> And cold so cold.

Mark felt he couldn't help but pity his grandmother. He hid his thoughts as he picked up a few sticks and last year's flowers, now decayed. Was there a spring of joy hidden within her? He suddenly wanted desperately to believe that there was a spring of joy ready to swell within the frail old woman. Yet, he could not. He was seeing tears in her eyes. Surely, tears are not the best portents of joy.

"Mark," she quavered, breaking the silence, "You'll be soon laying what is left of me here by your papa's side. He ended his life at peace with himself, with the world, and with God. It is the same with me. I am ready now, Mark. I was not ready before, but now I am ready."

Mark shuddered and a wave of sorrow passed over him. He couldn't speak, though his thoughts raced.

Grace continued, "You needed to hear me say this, Mark. Your mother told me about your interest in the poem framed and hung at the home. She saw you copying it down after the Nemo's program was over. Do you remember what the poem was all about, Mark? I understand what it says, because it is true about me. That's why I tell you that I am ready. Your papa wrote poems too, poems about God and heaven and eternity. But I never fully understood what he was trying to say. The Bible says that you have to have ears to hear. You can hear things without understanding them, but unless you understand them, you don't really hear it. Now I know what he and Mr. Nemo meant. And soon I'll be telling your papa that I understood in time to be prepared to go to him. Then he'll be even happier than he is now. I want you to be happy too, Mark. Like your mother, and me you were never happy. But your mother is happy now, and I am happy. Already Christ has redeemed my soul. My body is next."

Mark looked at Grace Targett's wrinkled face. Her tears falling from a smiling face were as a shower of rain on a sunny day. The joy was unaffected. That Mark knew. He realized at that moment he was not dealing with words only, that the substance of what they often failed to represent was there, devoid of pretense or poetical license. But he still found nothing to say. Mark took off his jacket and covered Grace's shoulders.

She murmured her thanks. Then, after a long, uninterrupted silence she continued, "Your papa left me some instructions about you before he died. It was not much, but for him it was very important. It's about his writings. Your father's abandonment of his family broke your papa's heart. His main concern was you. He knew that your tender heart was as broken as his was. He wanted desperately to mend it.

146

He told me that you might close your heart to any affection and rebel, or perhaps your suffering would make you into a caring person. As you grew up, I found out how right he was. You rebelled against all the past and shrank your ability to love."

"Have I been that bad, Granny?"

"It is possible that you do have love in your heart for people, but because your heart is closed, nobody knows it is there. It is like wrinkles, moans, and weakness hiding the joy of old people who have experienced redemption, as Mr. Nemo wrote in his poem. Your grandfather expected that some day you would be healed. I do see signs of healing in you of late. When you were healed, I was supposed to leave with you his writings. For many years, I felt bad that he was leaving you just words. Nothing of substance except the words he wrote. Mostly he wanted to be sure that I placed in your hands someday the manuscript of a book he had been working on. He died before he could finish it. I don't know how he knew that you would be a writer too. Your papa's writings were never published anywhere. He was a humble man—your papa was. I shall not live to see what you are going to do with the verbal heirloom he left for you in his will. He knew you would make good use of it. He had a bit of a prophet in him, you know."

Mark felt excitement surge through him. He heartily hoped his granny was not just using rambling words without truth, words that poured out of a mind no longer able to distinguish facts from fiction. Had Papa really thought that highly of a little six-year-old full of questions and mischief?

"There are more than just words in Grandfather's gift to me, Granny. I am sure I'll be richer from having it. I have lived with just the memory of Papa's soul. Now I shall be able to meet his soul again in the words that came from his heart."

Grace smiled at his eagerness. "I don't want to deliver my husband's writings to you in person, Mark. I thought it would be better if you found them yourself after I am gone. Do you remember the heavy trunk you and David were teasing me about when bringing it down from the attic? 'What do you have inside, Granny, gold?' That's what David said." Grace laughed, then continued, "I wanted to tell him that he guessed right. Inside that trunk are many pictures and mementos more precious to me than gold. Your grandfather's old suitcase where I placed all his writings is there too. Your mother will know what to do with the rest of the things you'll find in the trunk."

Grace reached for a pocket in the heavy cardigan dress she was wearing, and proceeded, "I'm leaving the key with you. I don't want anybody handling those papers before you have them with you. Now that my role in fulfilling your papa's wishes is over, I feel better prepared to meet him again. Come, dear Mark. Let us see a little bit more of the countryside where I grew up."

Mark put the trunk key in his pants' pocket. He was learning how sadness and joy could be present in one's heart at the same time. He gave grandmother his arm to lean on and together they walked toward his car. As the car nosed out of the cemetery, Grace asked, "Did you mean what you said, that you were giving me the whole day, when I asked you to take me for a ride? I wish I could see my old friend Norma before we go back. I know she is home now. Can you take me to her house?"

"Of course I can, Granny. I planned to give you the whole day. Do I know her?"

"You don't know her, Mark. We went to school together at the Lake Ariel High School. I was a year ahead of her. We have had good times together, skating on the lake in winter and talking about boys. I haven't been with her in a long time, Mark. We have many things to talk about. I am afraid you are going to be bored. You can just leave me there and come back for me later if you like. I am sure Norma wouldn't mind. But

I do want you to meet her. She's still a live wire and I love her dearly... I am sorry Mark; her house is in the other direction. I shouldn't be gabbing like this. Please turn around. Norma's house is in the other side of Route 196."

"No problem, Granny. There's a new library over in Hamlin. I have been meaning to look up a book I keep hearing about. I can go there and see if they have it. If they don't, there are plenty of other books to keep me occupied. Have you heard the name C. S. Lewis before, Granny?" Mark wanted to keep his grandmother talking. "I keep running across quotes from this writer and I have never read any of his works. How long do you need to stay visiting your friend? Do you want me to call you from the library?"

"Now you are rambling just like me. Yes, I am familiar with C.S. Lewis. Not a writer easy to read unless you are reading his children's books. I'll probably need a couple of hours, if you don't mind. Yes, take down Norma Kolesky's number and call before you come for me just in case."

By that time Mark had turned his little CRX around and was driving past the monastery and heading for Route 196. He was glad to be able to drive his grandmother around. And she had changed too. Everybody seemed to be changing, except him. Did he need changing too? Wouldn't that be a good question to ask Abby? He must see that little girl before he left town.

But what was most in Mark's mind was Granny Targett's great revelation about Papa. Mark had something to look forward to beyond a few months of cramming in Philadelphia and crime reporting in the fall.

Granny knew her way around. She told Mark who used to live here and who built that house over there after marrying so and so, who had gone to war, who died and who moved away. Grace Targett's mind was very much alive, though her body was failing. If only he had been as close to his Granny as he had been with his Papa.

CHAPTER 23

Words in a Cemetery

After Mark dropped his grandmother off at her friend's house, he changed his mind about going to the Hamlin library. He had thought vaguely of going back to his grandfather's grave though he couldn't give himself a reason for it. At the corner of Route 196, he turned left, impulsively. It was as if someone else was in charge of his vehicle. He drove again, slowly, past the monastery and pulled into the Canaan cemetery entrance. Another car was coming out. It was a silver Suzuki. Mark was pulling to his right to give the other car room to exit when he recognized the driver.

It was Abby! Mark could hardly conceal his joy. Abby had stopped her car past Mark's Honda. Mark backed his vehicle, placing it parallel to Abby's car. The drivers were face to face with each other.

"Do I know the young lady?" he asked teasingly.

"I shall be glad to introduce myself to the young gentleman, in case he doesn't. He looks harmless enough."

"Abby, I have wanted to see you. You're making yourself scarce lately. I'm supposed to be leaving town in two days and I dare not leave without a blessing from you. Can we talk?"

"Sure, Mark. I don't have my bottle of holy water with me, though. You will have to do without the blessing. But we can talk. I'll turn around and drive back in. Follow me then. There is a stone bench across from my family's plot. We can sit there and talk." Putting action into words, she accelerated her little car, turned around, and re-entered the cemetery. But not before she blew the horn in passing Mark's car just for effect. Mark followed her. Abby parked her car on the north side of the burial ground. By the time Mark stopped his vehicle behind her, Abby had already jumped out. Together they walked toward the bench still out of sight for him. The girl led. Mark followed.

"You come here often, Mark? I do. Not in winter much. I like to keep my dad's grave pretty and tidy."

"Probably not as often as you do. My grandfather is buried here too. I brought my grandmother to see his grave."

"And what did you do with your grandmother? I would have liked to see her again."

"She wanted to see an old friend of hers on the other side of Route 196. I left the two ladies to reminisce about old times by themselves. I am so glad I came back here just at the right time. I would have missed you if I hadn't."

Coming upon the stone bench Mark touched it with the palm of his hand. As he suspected, it was cold. He took off the winter jacket he had covered Grace Targett's shoulders with and stretched it on the stony seat.

Abby thanked him and they sat down. "And now who shall be the first to say what about what. Last time I saw you, you were eating ice cream at my house, and then you melted away. Seen some fiery dragon lately?"

"The girl is impossible," Mark thought, "I wonder what it would be like to be married to a little thunderbolt like that?" As quick as the bold thought flashed through his mind, it was dismissed.

"Sorry, Abby. I have not had time for dragons or dragonets lately. I have been busy closing up my apartment, helping my grandmother move from the house she sold and getting ready to go back to the university. Besides, I wanted to give my boss at the store as much work time as possible, not only to help him but to beef up my finances. It occurs to me that I never told you about my leaving the area—"

"No, you did not. Is this going to be a 'good-bye' or a 'see you later'?"

"See you later. I have now less than five months of grinding; then I'll be back here until the fall. That's when I should be writing for the *Scranton Daily* if they deliver on the promise of a job they made me."

"After that glossy write up on their future star reporter the other day I don't see how they can go back on their word. But I know you have set your eyes on higher goals than that."

"You're right. Journalism is my call. I love to write, but I don't intend to be writing about crime all my life. There's so much more to life than crime and courts. There are so many wrongs to correct, so many new solutions to the problems of human existence to find and try, so much needless suffering to alleviate. Yes, my aims are high."

"Mark, I am afraid you are not aiming high enough. I don't see you taking into consideration that we are created in God's own image. Our aspirations for fulfillment reach beyond matter, time, and earthly needs. No matter how much you do, you and those you want to serve will never be completely fulfilled. Redemption alone can bring completeness. And only God can provide that. I might sound to you as if I don't care for the world's problems and sufferings; that I, and others like me, go past human socio-economic ills on our way to eat our pie in the sky. That's not true, Mark. That's what your mentors and peers have been telling you. You can revise history, but you cannot revise truth. People who follow Christ care for the troubles of the world.

My grandfather, Mom's dad, was an educator who escaped your John Dewey's secularization of our education. Pappy was a world traveler. As a child, he would tell me that in all his travels he didn't come across a hospital in a non-industrialized country that had not been started by a missionary. That's when my interest in nursing was born. I wouldn't plan to be giving sick people baths and injections all my life, Mark, unless I aimed higher than gold or my patients' good. Sorry if I sound defensive and personal. But Mark, you don't see things the way they are. Don't you realize that your professors have robbed you of the only tool given to humanity to rightly distinguish good from evil? How can you discern what is good to be promoted or bad to be avoided? Goodness without God can easily turn out to be like poisoned food. Skeptics cannot leave people better off after leaving this world, Mark."

"I know that you think that I have been looking in the wrong direction in my aiming for the good of humanity. But, Abby, that's all I know for sure."

"And so much more that escapes your perception and mine. Mark, I admire you very much for wanting to right wrongs. I want that too, more than you know. But with your enthusiasm in crusading for good, you must know that you are not properly equipped for your mission. Your politically tinged education has done a terrible thing to you, Mark. Your mentors deny the fixity of truth's standard. Then they point to what they judge is wrong in the world and in our society basing their conclusions on theoretical, capricious premises, and prod you on to go out and correct it politically. They want you to fight your dragons with a stick and half a truth. A guessed truth, can often be more deadly than a lie. Mark, how can you properly identify what is truly good and what is truly bad without an accurate measure? It is young people so destitute of a fixed criterion that wrap explosives around their bodies and blow up themselves and others. They, too, think they are working and dying to accomplish good. I suspect that America's high sense of human value keeps our own crusaders from doing the same. As sensitive a person as you are, Mark, I am sure you can detect good transmuted into hate written on protesters' signs in the streets of America. I know that you don't hate America. I don't think you are good at hating. You are just—forgive me, Mark, if I sound insensitive, but I must say this. I don't think I might have another chance of being as open with you as I feel I must be. Believe me; I say it in deep concern. You have been brainwashed and you don't know it."

So blunt a statement could only be met with a revenging retort or with silence. Mark's response was silence. An emotion-filled silence surrounded the two youths so alike in their youthful vigor and altruism, yet worlds apart. The pause was long enough to allow Mark to mentally walk the dubious path he had followed in his life. His track of thought ended at the girl symbolizing all the good he had desired since his innocent days, a good plied out of his grasp by people claiming to know best of all who had lived before them. Was her diagnosis on the state of his mind accurate? Could he have been in darkness so far? Was he now finally seeing a ray of light coming from the soul and lips of a simple girl, younger, less experienced than he was? Words, words, words! Were they so heartless as to play their insensitive games with so guileless a soul as this girl's was?

Abby spent her silent time much differently. Her heart ached for the pain she had inflicted on her friend. The hurt was plainly visible on his honest face. She prayed as she fought tears. She knew that only Mark could break the silence. She could not. She should not. She dared not. But Mark could, and should and he dared.

"Abby, if my thinking has been manipulated, as you say, you need to do something for me. I love good; I love my country; and I am concerned with the world. I don't need deprogramming before I know that to be true. Tell me about America and good and the real world under the sunshine of the same reality that makes you so real to me." Mark was in earnest and the pain seemed to have lifted.

Abby paused for a moment, and then spoke as if reciting one of her favorite psalms. "America is a nation designed to be an anteroom from which her children who seek the utmost in justice and good—God—were to be ushered into another country—a permanent one. America is not an end. She is a transition. None of her political parties can do her any permanent good for now or for the future unless they realize this. That end is the supreme good from where all that is good in our country came from, all that made the period of transition more pleasurable. There is an eternity, Mark. Eternity is that point of infinity outside of the picture of the reality that we know. Eternity is what gives things their proper, believable shapes. It gives meaning to life. That point, of course, is God Himself. The Pilgrims knew this when they formed our nation. There are many who still believe that America is 'one nation under God.' But the number of those who fully accept and understand what that means is fast dwindling. Fewer people believe in our nation's God as our Creator, Who created man in His own image thus giving us his dignity and worthiness, with free will confirming those gifts. The ensuing freedom, never before experienced in any nation, led to greatness never before known. That's what is meant by America being a nation under God. If our country is to experience more good than evil and thus be preserved, Americans must understand and accept God as Creator, for freedom gives access to both, and only God can deal with the heart of evil." Abby paused.

Mark had willingly followed the thoughts so earnestly expressed. They were thoughts he had never heard articulated in his schoolbooks, from his teachers, or from anyone else.

"Where did you get those lofty thoughts, Abby? They are not in my history books."

"No! They are no longer found in most schoolbooks. The secret of our nation's greatness will be kept hidden by Americans who reject the founders' God. How can they talk about something they don't know and, if made to understand, refuse to believe? How are they to understand America's identity, her future, and her true role in the world? History depends mostly on words to pass truth in its integrality to new generations. You know, too, that words can be purposely omitted, added, or misinterpreted to mean what you want to be said. When you discard the template of truth by denying its source, God, truth and lie can become indistinguishable and thus ideologically irrelevant. That has been your diet since you learned to read and could understand what was being communicated to you in school and through the media. My lofty thoughts, as you put it, are not my own. The original founding documents of America have expounded them with enough clarity. And they echo the thoughts expressed in the Judeo-Christian Scriptures where the source of our culture lies. The Bible is the resource where our founders learned how the new nation should be conceived and kept. Those historical documents, and my Bible, were the texts my grandfather and teacher used to teach me how America came into being. They are the only reliable sources that can explain America's true identity. You have been denied both resources, Mark."

Mark thoughtfully weighed out his next words, "Your America is certainly a different America from the one I learned about. We seem to be talking about two different nations here."

"Yes, we are, Mark. When you realize that yours is not the real one, you'll find your efforts to help cure what ails her more successful." Abby stood up and took two steps toward her family's grave plot. She knelt and caressed the gravestone she had just cleaned that day from the smudges left there by the winter snow. Mark read the chiseled words beneath her fingers:

LT. GARY SWINGLE
U.S. Navy Aviator
Born March 2 1962.
Died for his Country August 10, 1991
There is peace now in his sky

"Mark," Abby finished, her voice trembling, "Your America is not the nation the Pilgrims came here to build; not the nation my Dad gave his life for." With these words, her emotions burst out of bounds.

Mark looked at the weeping girl and with her, he imagined an old man in his TV showroom, weeping also. Abby looked earnestly at him and said between sobs, "The America you know and serve is neither my father's nor my grandfather's America. Your America is 'The Other America'."

Mark stared at her, thinking of the three words he had so often repeated since September 11. His eyes were drawn, irresistibly, to another gravestone within her family plot that he had not noticed before, also swept and cleaned by loving hands. It read:

MARCO NEMO
Born Jan.15, 1921, Died—

CHAPTER 24

A Funeral

In Philadelphia, a week before graduation, Mark was heading down for breakfast when his telephone rang. It was his mother.

"Mark, Granny went to be with your papa during the night. Can you come right away? I need you, son." Helen's voice could not hide her grief. She had been crying.

"I'll leave right away, Mom. Please, take it easy."

"Thank you, Mark. I'll have your room ready for you. Drive carefully, son!"

The news was no surprise. He had been expecting it. A little ray of light flickered in the midst of the darkness of sadness descending suddenly over his heart. Mother called him *son*, and the word had sounded just like when he had heard it in his innocence for the first time. Mark knew she meant it this time. Mother wanted to be motherly now. That is how he had always wanted her to be. Changes. Everything changes. Good and bad changes. If only all changes were good. How can death, the most momentous of all changes bring good? What was that Bible verse Abby quoted in her last e-mail? "All things work together for good to those who love God" or something like that. Mark still had much to learn what love, that flirtatious little word, really meant. And how could he direct the feeling he didn't understand toward Someone who was unknowable? Marco Nemo's granddaughter had been patient with him. That girl was for real. There was not much that was for real in the world. Mark doubted Abby would change. Abby didn't need to change. If she ever did, would the change be for the bad? He found himself longing to see her again. Would she know about Granny Targett?

Mark was lost in his musing while packing the few things he would need while with his mother. Thoughts of his mother and Abby were welcome, but not thoughts of his dear grandmother. Suddenly, a sense of loss overwhelmed him and he dropped to the bed, hid his head in his hands, and wept. Was he crying for himself or for Granny? Where was she? At rest? In Heaven? With God? Was there a God?

After a few minutes, he recovered himself, went over to the telephone, and punched in a number he knew by heart. After four rings, the answering machine announced its readiness to receive a message. Mark wavered between leaving a sad message in the care of insensitive chips and hanging up. But his urge to share his grief won over.

"Abby, this is Mark. I am about to leave Philly for Mother's house in Galilee. It is about Grandmother Grace. I just got a call to say she died last night. I would like to see you, Abby. I need you to tell me how Granny's death can work out for good. Please, don't tell me you don't know. There's nothing you don't know. I'll see you, Abby."

When all was in readiness for him to leave, and one final check in his valise's inner pocket assured him he still had the trunk key, which would unlock the gold of his grandfather's words that was to be his inheritance, he ate. Breakfast was forgotten as he drove north. He should be in Galilee by noon.

Next to the actual death of a family member, the saddest moment was the taking of the lifeless body out of the home.

Mark was spared that. It was Helen who held back the door and her tears as the stretcher went past the front entrance and into the waiting hearse. Granny Grace was never again to pass through it. This scene is one of the many in the course of experiencing death where the word finality craves for human attention. Callousness and skepticism can do nothing to counter it; nothing can seal its lips. Its hoarse voice is heard in every measured gesture toward the disposing of what was once all we could see of the human being. And the final few hours would leave nothing but memories which, though pleasant if the dead had been loved, were still cloaked in sadness and, often, in many tears.

That was the first time Mark faced the death of a relative as an adult. When one is no longer a child, the feeling is complicated by the maturity of reasoning. And death itself does not define its role in reality. Each person must either inject his own interpretation of it or ignore it altogether until it comes for him too. Mark had yet to learn how to live contentedly with death at his heels.

Helen was home alone when Mark came through the door. He was just in time to see his mother break into uncontrollable weeping. She had been trying to tidy up the room where her mother had breathed her last. Awkwardly, he hugged her tight and let her sob until she felt relieved. When had he last hugged his mother? His own eyes were only moist. He had already had his cry.

Later, subdued, mother and son went over the plans for the funeral. Grace Targett had made her wishes known about how she wanted to be buried. It was to be simple. No fancy coffin. The pastor who had baptized her after her recent conversion was to officiate in the service. She had already asked Norma Kolesky to sing. Grace had made sure of that the day she and Mark had gone together for a ride in the countryside. Norma still could sing, with feeling and with a pleasant, humble voice though trembly under the weight of age. Even the song had been picked. The two ladies had cried, laughed, and prayed together as they went over the words of the hymn. They were both glad to know Grace was finally prepared to die.

In the evening Abby called. She had gotten Mark's telephone message half an hour before, upon returning from the hospital. She needed to know the plans for the viewing and interment. Abby wanted to be there. Then she paused, and added, "Mark, I spent a long time talking with your mother the other day while visiting an old friend at the Pocono Home. I fell in love with her. What is more, she told me your grandmother was spiritually prepared to die. Your mother herself led her to faith last winter. I don't think you are prepared to know how meaningful that is. I do, Mark, and I am glad for your Mom and her mother. You said in your telephone message that I know everything. We both know, of course, that that's not true. I am just blessed with knowing what is important to know about life and death, time and eternity. That I can share with you, Mark."

There was that word faith again. The religion-coined word seemed to be passed around so easily, so often. Its outside was too worn out to try to identify its tendering value. 'Intelligent faith,' that's how Abby once tried to clarify its meaning for Mark. But to him even that needed clarification.

"Abby, I still have to go back to Philly after this. Would you be able to spend some time with this infidel before I leave again?"

"Sure, Mark. I'll rearrange my schedule to do that. Maybe right after the funeral. It would be good if your mother and the two of us ride back to her house after all is over. Check with her about that. She might want to be alone after an exhausting day. Or we can make other plans. We'll talk again at the funeral home. You'll be busy talking to people there. You'll have to look me up in the crowd."

Three days later Helen and Mark rode to Honesdale for

the funeral on a warm June afternoon. Mark was driving his mother's car. Behind the small funeral home on Main Street, Mark parked the car in the lot yet empty of vehicles. They had been instructed by the funeral director to be there half an hour before the service started. The viewing and the service would be combined. Grace had wanted it to be that way. Mark and Helen were to be told then what to expect and how to position themselves in the chapel.

After the three of them finished talking and a few people were about to start filing in to sign the guest book, Mark wandered by the coffin. Granny Grace's peaceful looking face contrasted with the grief-bathed one he remembered breaking the news to him, an angry six-year-old boy, that his papa was in heaven. Again, he recalled that Papa had a smile on his face when he died. "Papa must have had that illusive thing called faith," Mark thought as he moved toward the sea of flowers surrounding the coffin. He wished he had been old enough then to learn about faith from him.

Next to the coffin on a lighted stand, Mark saw a gold framed plaque. He recognized the eight-by-ten frame as the same kind he had seen at the Pocono Home's visitor lounge with Marco Nemo's poem in it. But this picture had a two-window mat. One window showed colorful, wild flowers, pressed, dried, and artistically arranged together. In the other was a song taken right out of a church hymnbook. It was titled "Be Still My Soul." The music was credited to Sibelius and the text to someone called Katharina von Schlegel. Mark read the lyrics between the two staves of written music:

> *Be still, my soul! The Lord is on thy side;*
> *Bear patiently the cross of grief or pain;*
> *Leave to thy God to order and provide;*
> *In every change He faithful will remain.*
> *Be still, my soul! Thy best, thy heavenly Friend*
> *Thro' thorny ways leads to a joyful end.*

Be still, my soul! Thy God doth undertake
To guide the future as He has the past.
Thy hope, thy confidence let nothing shake;
All now mysterious shall be bright at last.
Be still, my soul! The waves and winds still
   know
His voice who ruled them while He dwelt below.

Be still, my soul! The hour is hastening on
When we shall be forever with the Lord,
When disappointment, grief, and fear are gone,
Sorrow forgot, love's purest joys restored.
Be still, my soul! when change and tears are
   past,
All safe and blessed we shall meet at last.

Mark was moved. The word faith never appeared in the flowing rhythm of the masterfully written poem. Could the powerful force behind this moving hymn of confidence be what Abby means by faith? And there was this thing about change during which 'God faithful will remain.' Mark remembered Abby saying that faith is a gift from God, evidently the faithful God of the poet. It directly answered Mark's challenge to show how the change death brings could be a good thing. Was that girl behind this?

She was. Mark had just enough time before he would have to position himself by the coffin with his mother to read the card attached to the plaque: "*In loving Memory of Grace Targett, from Abigail Swingle.*" Just then, the funeral director came to take him to where his mother was already standing, ready to receive the condolences of friends. The room was filling.

What Mark just read kept running through his mind as people filed before mother and son, shaking hands with them, saying encouraging words to them. Mark didn't know most of the people. He decided they were probably people from the church his mother and Granny attended. Abby was one of the last in line. She hugged Helen for a long time. Then she turned to Mark. She hugged him too. He had wished she would do that. Abby seemed to have a sense of what was required of her. And she was always ready to give.

"Hold on, Mark dear," Abby encouraged, before walking over to the coffin. "We'll have this last dragon beat yet."

As Grace Targett had instructed, the service was a simple one. Pastor Brown told her friends and relatives how that he had the opportunity of attesting to Grace's preparedness to meet God. His message exuded faith and contentment based on a sure hope of better things in the afterlife. When he was finished, Norma Kolesky stood up to sing. There was no accompaniment. Her tremulous voice was warm and moving. Her words were clearly enunciated. She sang:

> Be still, my soul! The Lord is on thy side;
> Bear patiently the cross of grief or pain;
> Leave to thy God to order and provide;
> In every change He faithful will remain.
> Be still, my soul! Thy best, thy heavenly Friend
> Thro' thorny ways leads to a joyful end....

She sang all three verses. By the time Norma Kolesky finished the song many people in the audience were wiping tears. Mark gained control of his own emotions by wondering whether the singer and Abby were together in the choice of song.

He was going to ask her about it in the evening.

CHAPTER 25

Hounded

A bby had followed Helen's car as they made their way back to the house. The sun was already descending over the mountains when both cars filed into Helen's driveway. She unlocked the front door with Abby at her side while Mark searched for something in the back of his mother's car.

"Thank you, Abby, for coming home with us." Helen said. "It means a lot to me. I—"

"I am glad I could do it, Mrs. Cummings. Are you sure you are not too exhausted to have company?"

"I do feel tired, Abby. Tired and somewhat numb. But my soul is stilled. The song Norma sang was such a soothing balm. Please, don't worry about me. I think Mark is the one who needs you. He hides his feelings well."

Mark climbed the steps to the door. "Mr. Conway put this package on the back seat of the car saying it was a present from someone. I wonder what it is and who this someone happens to be." Mr. Conway was the funeral director. Mark knew well what was in the package and who the gift giver was. He was just preparing the stage to ask Abby whether she and Norma Kolesky had been conspiring.

After they were comfortably seated on the living room couch, Mark lifted the gift-wrapped package from his lap. From the white card attached to it he read, "*To be delivered to Mark Targett after the service. Thank you.*" The lettering was unmistakably Abby's. As he unwrapped the picture, Mark said, with a hint of a tease, "You are a bad girl, Abby. You didn't have to do this. And did you have a hand in picking the song for Norma Kolesky to sing?"

Abby looked serious, "I really needed to have that song framed and placed among the flowers by Granny's coffin. The hymn came to my mind the moment I heard your message on the phone that day. You wanted me to tell you how good can come out of death, remember? I cannot think of a better introduction to this subject than what the lyrics in the song say. As for Norma Kolesky, I don't know her. I did try to catch her after the service before she left. I wanted to ask her myself why she picked 'Be Still My Soul' for her solo, but she was already gone."

Mark could not reply. He remembered the Bible verse on deception and how he had asked Abby how many books there were in the Bible. He asked, wonderingly, "Abby, how many hymns are there in your hymn book?"

"Many hundreds. Thousands if you include all the different hymn books." She answered absently, then turned to him. "Are you familiar with *The Hound of Heaven* by Francis Thompson? I often think of that unusual work and its writer when I think about you. You should know by now that you are being hounded. Not by me. All I have been doing is praying that you stop running."

In the ensuing silence, Mark's wonder at the hymn choice by two separate parties was momentarily offset by such an intriguing title.

As if she had read into his thoughts, Abby continued, "The author's life is even more interesting than the book. He was an Englishman and a true genius. For years he lived in the streets, unable to fit his powerful intellect into the day-to-day business of living. British publishers vied for his writings done between bouts with opium. He would leave his writings in the newspapers' mailboxes without identifying himself. 'There is a genius among us', publishers would say, 'and no one knows who he is.' Nobody was able to enter his complex world to rescue him. Then one day he came across the words of Christ—His claims to be God come in the flesh to redeem mankind—and he believed and was converted. It was almost too late for him, but not too late for him to write *The Hound of Heaven*, a religious classic about the unrelenting way with which God seeks those 'who are to be heirs of salvation', as the Bible puts it. Francis Thompson is one of the many people in my long list of individuals I am looking forward to chatting with in heaven."

Again, there was a moment of silence as Mark meditated on what he had just heard. Had that author been entangled with words, like himself? The word he was dueling with right then was 'faith'. Intelligent faith, as Abby had qualified the word.

"Abby," he said finally, "you said before that faith is a gift from God. How can the Divine Hunter give the hounded something while the quarry is running for its life?"

"The quarry will have to stop, Mark. That's what I have been praying for you to do. That's where intelligence comes in, when the prey is endowed with such a gift. I learned this as a toddler while running after a baby robin in our back yard. The little thing had a broken wing. I wanted so desperately to hold him in my hands, love him, and try to mend his wings so he could fly again. But he didn't know it and I had no way of telling him. I sat on the grass and cried as the robin kept running further and further away from me. My heart broke when I saw a hawk dive, pounce on my little friend, and fly away with him. It was a traumatic experience for me, Mark. As you can see, I still cry when I remember it." Abby dabbed at her eyes.

Helen came in from the kitchen with a tray.

"Here, kids. You have a choice of tea or coffee. I didn't want to interrupt you to ask so I brought what you needed for either one. The cookies are homemade. Norma Kolesky brought them to us. Don't let me interrupt you again. I'll be in the dining room if you need me." She laid the tray on the coffee table and left.

"Tell me, Abby," Mark wondered, after Helen had left the room, "What can the prey do to stop running? It is not easy when running is an instinctive thing to do."

"The figure of speech should be understood as just that—a figure of speech. In reality, no one can run away from God for He is everywhere. As theologians describe this divine attribute, God is Immanent and Omnipresent. People don't instinctively run away from God. Not the real God. That is impossible. The naturalistic meaning of the word instinct is not in God's theological vocabulary. You have been running from a set of proud ideas about a non-existing God, which a few over-self-confident, rebellious intellectuals concocted. The impetus for such ideas could have come from the wide acceptance of the theory of evolution. As you have experienced, this mutinous concept of God is being forced into our Western culture mostly through education and the media. You are among millions of well-educated Americans victimized by the dialectical material-ism leading them to death. No civilization without the right concept of God can last. That's why we are seeing our Western civilization being dismantled before our eyes. And, Mark, though you mean well as so many in our generation do, you are contributing to that end. And you'll be destroy-ing your own soul while doing it."

"I have to think about all this, Abby. You have given me more than I can take with one bite. Do you own a copy of *The Hound of Heaven*? I would like to read it."

"My copy is with a friend, the same one who has my Frost book. You might find it in a bookstore. I am sure you'll be able to find it in a good library. Meanwhile I'll see if Lynn is finished with it. When do you have to go back to Philadelphia?"

"I am leaving early in the morning. I'll be back in a few days."

Abby got up from the couch. "Your mother seemed very tired and has been alone all evening. I think I should go to her before I leave. I would like to pray with her." She turned at the door to add, "You look tired too. You'd better rest for your trip tomorrow. I'll find my way out after visiting with your Mom."

CHAPTER 26

A Manuscript and the Word

Mark didn't retire after Abby left him. He climbed to the attic while checking for the trunk key he had kept in his pocket all day. The trunk was still where he and David had placed it a few months earlier when they had moved Grandmother Targett's things. Mark pulled the trunk closer to the light and placed an old footstool in front of it. He had told his mother before about Granny's inheritance so he didn't feel that he was intruding. He sat awkwardly on the small piece of furniture, inserted the key, and tried the old locker. It opened without resistance.

The strong smell of mothballs was the first thing Mark noticed. Everything was neatly arranged inside the trunk. There were boxes and folders filled with faded pictures from the early twentieth century, as he could tell by their clothing. He found clips of writings that had seemed important to someone, knick-knacks of dubious value and need in our day and age, old magazines deemed worth keeping—all the mementos that attested to the unrelenting passing of time. In one side of the trunk, loosely laid by numerous other items, Mark saw what he was looking for. It was a valise that looked much like his own, but older. He lifted it, ceremoniously, out of the trunk, placed it on his lap, and carefully opened the lid. Another waft of mothballs escaped from the valise. Grandmother had been determined to preserve its content.

As Mark expected, the valise contained only papers, some typed, and some with handwritten notations. A thick folder held many pages of poems. He hoped Grandfather Targett wrote them all. Another large folder contained letters. He bypassed the letters and turned back to the poems. He read one or two. What a treasure! Years melted away, and he could almost feel the dear presence of his grandfather. How he longed to read them all. But they would have to wait. He picked up the thickest of the folders. This one interested him most. On the cover was written:

> *AMERICA! AMERICA!*
> *(A Tentative Title)*

On the first page as he opened the folder, Mark read:

> *Dedicated to my little grandson, Marky,*
> *who inherited my name, and, hopefully,*
> *the principles that made our nation great,*
> *lest his children grow up in an America our*
> *founders never conceived.*

Mark's emotions in reading this were impossible to describe. For a long time he sat there, looking at the folder and wishing its whole content of ideas could be instantly downloaded into his mind, like in a computer. At the same time, he felt he should take time to savor this morsel of the past. He was going to be acquainted with Papa's soul—finally. Mark suddenly felt his life would have been incomplete without this revelation and that it was too sacred a thing for him to rush into. He would wait until the time was right and his mind was free from other preoccupations.

Mark carefully rearranged the contents of the valise, placed it back in the trunk, closed the lid carefully, and locked it again. He moved the trunk and the stool back to where they were before and descended the stairs. He turned off the light and carefully closed the attic entrance. He didn't want to disturb the girls.

But Abby was already gone. Mark looked at his watch. It was 11:30. There was still a light in the living room. His mother was sitting where he had sat talking with Abby. She had her Bible precariously opened on her lap. Helen had fallen asleep. Mark was about to retrace his steps so as not to disturb his mother when she woke up with a long sigh.

"Mark, dear, is that you?"

Mark knelt beside this woman who seemed dearer to him than she ever had. "You OK, Mom?" He felt almost anxious for her, seeing lines on her face he had not noticed before.

"I am all right, son. I am glad your girl friend came to see us. Where in the world have you found such a jewel, Mark?"

"I have not found Abby. She found me. You are right. She is a precious girl. She has been good to me. You should be in bed now, Mother."

"You ought to be resting too, Mark, for your long ride tomorrow."

Mark, tired as he was physically and emotionally, had little sleep that night. For a long time he lay in bed, thinking. He had to restrain himself from going back to the attic; he longed to experience the imprint of Papa's soul on his own soul. He sensed that the contents of Granny's trunk were going to be a turning point in his life. But he needed to take stock of his life first. He had to be prepared for changes. Mark was learning that changes are steps on the ladder of life. One should use ladders carefully. He needed to evaluate the rung he was stepping on and be sure the next step was up, not down. He wanted to climb to the same plateau of contentment and peace his papa had known. When Mark did fall asleep, he dreamed of Papa stretching down his hand to little Marky from his lofty place, urging the child to climb up and be with him.

In the morning as he drove down the Pennsylvania turnpike Mark mused that his 'new' mother would not have let him out of the house knowing he had so little sleep. He was tired, but alert. His mind was working clearly. In three more days Mark would be back home. He was looking forward to freedom from textbooks and essays. He was going to immerse himself in his grandfather's thoughts without any constraints of time. Helen wanted him to stay with her at least until he was ready for his Scranton job. Mark was glad for that.

With all Mark had to tie up at school before graduation day those three days went by quickly. He was not much for ceremonies and looked to his graduation day with dread. But when his name was called and he walked up to the podium to receive his diploma the occasion took on new meaning for him. On the third row of the audience seats, he spotted the beaming faces of Abby and his mother. They were waving and applauding. Then, after the ceremony was over Helen and Abby met him at the exit. Two hugs and two heartfelt congratulations warmed his heart.

Mark had his CRX packed full and ready to go. The only space left in the two-seater was the one to be occupied by the driver. His mother had driven her car down and Abby rode with her. He would have liked to have Abby ride with him. He thought of suggesting his mother drive his car while he drove hers, but then remembered that Helen had never learned to shift gears. Mark would have to be alone on the two and a half hour drive north.

Mark let his mother lead with her car. He was expecting to see her take the road to Bethany to drop Abby off at home, but they drove toward Galilee. When they entered Helen's home, he found out why Abby was still with them. The girls had a welcome home party arranged for him. Though only the three of them participated, there were balloons and a pompously decorated cake on the table. The room was garnished with flowers and party decorations. But above all, there were two warm human beings that were glad to be with him on this important day of his life. It was late in the evening when he watched a tired Abby drive away.

Mark helped Helen to finish tidying up the room before they stopped for the day. He was eagerly anticipating delving into his grandfather's writings. For the last three days, this had become almost an obsession with him.

He refused his mother's offer to help him unload his little car. She had done enough, he said. It was almost midnight before both of them could go to sleep. It had been a happy but tiring day.

Mark's mother had prepared Granny Targett's former room for him. She had even placed a Bible on the nightstand. Mark smiled when he noticed it and was surprised to feel a warm appreciation for it. He picked up the brown leather book and opened it. The dedicatory read: *"To Mark, on his graduation, praying that The Word will turn his love-hate relationship with words into love only. In Jesus' Love, Abigail Swingle."* Mark puzzled over the girl's meaning. Under her signature she wrote, "John 1:3-18."

Abby had not wrapped the present. Mark didn't fail to observe this. And the meaning was clear—a Bible is more than a thing to be given, too important a book not to be quickly available. Just like Abby. As he put the Bible back on the nightstand, he noticed a small hardbound booklet on top of his dresser. *The Hound of Heaven* was the title. Abby must have gotten her book back from her friend.

Abby's dedicatory note was still in his mind. Had he ever talked with her about his long-standing love-hate relationship with words? Or had the girl guessed it? Was he to find healing of this duplicity in the Bible? Though less concerned lately about this condition, he still couldn't think of a word, concrete or abstract, that was in itself the very substance it was supposed to represent. He still felt he needed to receive the healing Abby was praying about.

Mark fought his intense desire to go right back to Grandfather's manuscript before retiring for the day for he intended to relish every sentence his papa wrote. For this, he wanted his mind fresh and clear. Mark got dressed for the night and lay in bed, ready to give himself a full night's sleep. As he reached to flick off the nightstand light, he saw the Bible again. What was it that Abby wrote under her signature? He picked up the Bible again and reread the reference she had written down: *John 1:3-18*. Curiously, he turned the pages of the Book. Where would he find John?

On the third page of the Bible, he spotted a table of contents. *"John, Gospel of,"* he read, *"page 1515."* Mark propped himself up in bed as he turned to the page, located the spot and started to read. His attention was grabbed by the first words. The section of the chapter was entitled by the editors, *The Word Became Flesh*. Enthralled by the caption, he read:

> *In the beginning was the Word, and the Word was with God, and the Word was God. The same was in the beginning with God. All things were made by Him; and without Him was not any thing made that was made. In Him was life; and the life was the light of men. And the light shineth in darkness; and the darkness comprehended it not.*

Mark had never before read anything like this. He paused in astonishment. Was this poetry? Was the Bible involved in linguistics too? Who was this Him? Mark read on.

There was a man sent from God, whose name was John. The same came for a witness, to bear witness of the Light, that all men through him might believe. He was not that Light, but was sent to bear witness of that Light. That was the true Light, which lighteth every man that cometh into the world. He was in the world, and the world was made by Him, and the world knew Him not. He came unto His own, and His own received Him not. But as many as received Him, to them gave He power to become the sons of God, even to them that believe on his name: Which were born not of blood, nor of the will of the flesh, nor of the will of man, but of God. And the Word was made flesh, and dwelt among us... full of grace and truth... No man hath seen God at any time; the only begotten Son, which is in the bosom of the Father, He hath declared Him.

His tiredness was gone. Mark devoured the book of John, well past the verses Abby had indicated. He read the whole Gospel. Still hungry for more, he turned to the first book, Genesis, wanting to take in the whole Bible from the beginning. Under the editors' title *The Creation*, Mark started to read:

In the beginning God created the heavens and the earth. And the earth was without form, and void; and darkness was upon the face of the deep. And the Spirit of God moved upon the face of the waters. And God said, Let there be light: and there was light...

Mark had to stop there for a moment. What he had just found out was too radical a thought for him to pass by. A world created with words! God didn't manufacture anything. He didn't make a magic pass and—bang! There it was. He created the world with words—words! God said, *"Let there be..."* he read the words again, *"and it was so."* What a fascinating thought!

Mark read on. Seven times, he counted; Genesis reported that God spoke things into creation. All things, except humankind. *"Let us make man in our image, after our likeness..."* Mark read in verse twenty-six. Questions kept surging into his mind as he continued to read.

Around three in the morning, Helen woke up and saw light in Mark's room. The door was open. She tiptoed in. Mark was sprawled on the bed, the Bible still open in his motionless hand. He was fast asleep. Helen gently took the Bible from his hand and placed it on the nightstand. She turned off the light and stood for a long time looking tenderly at her son.

CHAPTER 27

Papa's Preface

Mark awakened with the sun's morning brightness pouring through the window's white curtain. He had forgotten to pull the shade down. He looked at his watch. It was past nine. All was quiet in the house. The revelatory learning experience of the night came again full force into his mind fully awake. Where had he been all this time? "This is solid stuff," he thought to himself. Then he remembered Abby. "So that's the book that girl loves! Now I can see why."

It was so quiet in the house. Was mother still there? Had she told him anything about leaving? Checking in the kitchen and his mother's room revealed nothing. Looking out the window, he saw that his car was alone in the driveway. Finally, he found a note on the bathroom mirror.

> *"I am leaving for work, Son. Will be gone all day. There's plenty of cereal in the closet and bread in the breadbox. Milk's in the refrigerator. Spaghetti too. Coffee and sugar on the counter. I am so glad you are with me, Mark. Love, Mother."*

"Ah, the house to myself." Quiet and undisturbed, he would pursue what he had held before him as a carrot on a stick—his grandfather's writings! On the other hand, the Bible seemed to fascinate him as well. Should he—? Then Mark smiled. "Changes. There have been plenty of them of late. All things working together for good.... Where can I find that in the Bible, now that I have one?" He found himself wavering between the two choices. The manuscript won for the time being.

Mark had a quick bowl of cereal in the kitchen and set the automatic coffee brewer. He brought down the old valise from the attic, placed it on the kitchen table, and took the manuscript out. He bypassed the dedicatory and concentrated on the introduction which his grandfather entitled *"Preface."*

One of the weaknesses of the human mind is its proneness to take the container for the content. This can be a prelude to disappointments and, often, danger. It is due to this that advertisers and merchants invest much thought and money to find out how best to package their products to maximize profits.

Right after the Second World War the number of babies born with physical deformities increased noticeably in the Middle East. A team of American medical researchers was brought in to discover why this was happening in that particular area. Their findings: willful, criminal packaging. Unwary families were using oil for their cooking out of cans labeled as olive oil. But some enterprising businessmen were mixing cooking oil with motor oil left behind by the American troops. The deadly mixture was sold in familiar cans labeled as pure olive oil.

The properly uniformed man pumping insecticide throughout the bank's building could be the bank robber who is planning to burglarize it. The flag-waving, Bible-toting politician could be the one who willfully or ignorantly destroys his country. The only way to identify a true American is to know who America really is and match words and intentions with her true identity. To fail to know who America really is, is to condemn our nation to slow extinction through the actions of those who do not love her, or who only think they do.

For many years, America has been losing her identity. Only a few people even realize it. This nation has many enemies, both within and without. The foe is ready to use our misperception to weaken and destroy our nation. Ours is a democratic republic where the government is chosen out of its people, by its people. For this reason, it is vital that the majority of us know the true identity of America. 'The puzzle that is America,' as the hero of my true story calls the picture of America as it is placed before Americans and the world, must be put together correctly if we are to survive as a nation.

A nation is defined by her people. God told Abraham, the founder of the other nation 'under God', "I will make of thee a great nation." The Man Jesus whose teachings set the foundation for our Western civilization taught us "as a man thinketh in his heart, so is he." What makes an individual is what makes his country, because individuals make a nation. The principles governing a successful human being are the same principles governing a successful nation.

The life story of Nande Carmo is a parable of America. In his desire to "put the puzzle that is America" together, he came across the principles that made America great. By applying those principles to his life, he succeeded as a human being the same way America succeeded as a nation. Significantly, like our historical Pilgrims, Nande was already seeking to abide by those principles even before learning to articulate them.

A few principled people whose spirituality became the

183

dominant genes that were to make this nation what she became carved America out of adversity. A concerned American in the jungle of the country where Nande was born sacrificially shared those same spiritual principles. Natives there faced the same adversities our founders encountered on our shores when they conceived America. Nande Carmo came to understand those principles, applied them, timidly at first, and saw the proven fruits in his own successful life. As for his own nation's success, all he could do was pray. He found out that America couldn't be simply emulated. In his own words, "It can only come by birth or rebirth." This lesson had almost cost Nande his life.

Professor Carmo told me his story himself. Like the First Comers, as the Quakers called the Pilgrims, he spoke English with a foreign accent. But as a late coming Pilgrim to America, Nande arrived on our shores moved by the same spirit possessed by the men and women sailing on the Mayflower. He succeeded in life as America succeeded as a nation not because he learned to emulate our nation's ethos. He succeeded because he learned who the first comers were and became like one of them.

By the time I met Nande Carmo, the fear of hunger and of jungle beasts, and of oppressive government and bondage was long gone from him. But there was a nagging, growing fear in his America-loving heart. He feared for the future of our nation, now his nation. And so do I. We have seen the changes that have taken place in America in the last fifty years. Baneful changes—out of character with America—threaten to do away with our nation, throw her glory in the dust, and redefine her in the light of other nations. There is a growing cultural dementia in our country. Like an Alzheimer patient, today's America does and says things the America of our founders would never do or say. As this nation has brought prosperity and freedom to her and to the world, she might also, in her insanity, lead the Western civilization to self-destruction. East and west are bound to confront each other in a decisive battle for the soul of mankind. America can still save our civilization once again. But only if in full possession of her true identity.

Hear the parable of America taken from the true story of a twentieth century Pilgrim. It echoes back to us from the culturally pristine jungle where this nation, through her goodness, and missionaries who followed Jesus, had shown herself for what she really was. Through the words and lives of some of her God-fearing children, she taught primitive men God's design for humans and nations. May we still have ears to hear, hearts to understand, and wills to be healed.

The preface was signed by Mark Targett, and was dated in June of 1984.

Mark stood up and stretched fascination in his mind and expectation in his heart. He felt that he was on the verge of a life-changing discovery, that he would never be the same again. He remembered learning in his college days that he would be the same in ten years except for the people he met and the books he read. Mark suspected that Papa's manuscript was about to impact his thinking and his life—forever.

Part Two

CHAPTER 28

The Forgotten Name

*T*he sun was just rising over the jungle when the young Indian started for the village. He was in his mid-twenties. It would be more than a full day's trip. His oxcart wheels were already engrossed in their monotonous, squeaky song in minor key. The oxen's five-mile-an-hour strolling added to the dolefulness of the wheels' dirge.

The young man had an important duty to perform that day in the village besides taking the watermelons he carried in the cart. Today he would exchange them for kerosene and sugar. Mother wanted some denim for clothing if he had enough watermelons. They often had to do without any of those things not found in the jungle. They had done without clothing before. They could do it again. It didn't really matter.

His other errand had to be done no matter the cost or effort. His latest child had arrived into his bleak world the week before. A boy. The midwife said the baby would live so he must register him in the village's government office. The current dictator needed to know how many soldiers he could command, even eighteen years in advance. The dictator wanted to be in charge for the rest of his life, like a king. With the infant mortality in the country being so high, two out of five living, three dying, all had to be counted. The shaky seat of total power needs a strong statistical ground to stay put. For the oxcart driver that was child number five. Two had already died at birth without names. You didn't pick names for children until you knew that they would stay alive. Illiterate and away from civilization, he didn't know that, so far, he had been able to beat the grim odds.

As he traveled, he kept repeating the name the baby had been given. "Darius," the wife had said. "We'll call him Darius." She looked happy saying that. She had heard the name from the lips of the funny sounding American missionary reading the Bible. Darius was a king a long, long time ago, he had told them. The name sounded good to her ears. But they had never heard it before. The father was afraid he would forget it. To keep it in his mind and to pass the time, he started to say the word in time with the cart wheels' sound as a counterpoint to their chanting. Squeak. Darius! Squeak (pause). Squeak. Darius! Squeak (pause)—

By noon, he was not yet halfway to his destination, and he was hungry. He ate his manioc flour and dried meat fried in pork fat, and then drank from the spring by the trail leading to the village. The sun was blazingly hot overhead, but for now, he had the shade of a tree to stop under and rest. The oxen were munching contentedly, and resting too. It would be so good to just stay there a while and take a siesta. But he had to go on before the darkness overtook him. There was the danger of wild animals too. Got to move on. Got to remember the baby's name. The baby's name! He suddenly realized that the sound of the strange name was gone from his head. It was as if it existed only in between the squeaks of the cart's wheels motionless, silent.

Even after the oxen were again slowly pulling the cart along, the baby's name continued buried somewhere in the father's mind. And he had to keep going further and further away from his hut. And mother was the only other person, *besides the missionary, who could remind him of the name. He experimented with sounds, in the hope of fishing the baby's name out of his head. But what he could come up with in the renewed singsong of the wheels sounded even stranger to him than the missing word. Torius. Barius. Clarius. It could be any of those. But how was he to know for sure? By the time he pulled the oxcart up by the government office in the village he had given up remembering.*

"Sir," he questioned, "We have this baby boy born a week ago. We ain't got a name for him yet. I mean, we do have one picked out. But I just can't remember what it is. Can you find a name for a little, squealing, baby boy?" The government man smiled condescendingly. Then he picked up an ink pen and wrote a name down while answering the father's question. "Nande," he recited, and proceeded with the formality.

And Nande it remained to this day. The name is to be written on a tombstone somewhere in a civilized American cemetery someday. That is where Nande Carmo lives now, all traces of jungle, ignorance, and penury gone out of his life.

Only those who invest their lives in eternity by investing them in others know how they become liaisons between people and God. They change lives, not only in matters of the soul, but in matters of the body also. This is even more so in the jungles. The One Who sends them on their mission there once multiplied bread. Missionaries quickly learn to multiply for themselves and for those in their care their meager substance of food and comfort. They must pull an infected tooth, keep alive a starving baby, teach a mother how to sew and a father how to dig a well with the basic ingredients of civilized know-how. With generous giving back home, a small jungle clinic is often started, to become the best and, many times, the only hospital for miles around.

With the charity goes this message: "Life is short, eternity is long. Sin degrades life here and shuts the door to a better and eternal life. But like the air we breathe, redemption is free. Free to us, that is. Someone had paid for it in full. His name is God. He paid the price not as God, but in the form of a man. It cost Him His life. One can take the gift and live here in hope and in eternity fully happy, or refuse it and die in want. This condition is common to all human beings, from the headhunter to the university professor. The Giver also gives to us all the dignity of a choice, for He created man in His own image."

The Stanleys had told the Carmos all that and had showed them the way to implement those truths into their lives. Five years after Nande arrived, pills and quinine were not saving his mother's life. The Stanleys diagnosed her health problem as beyond their ability to help, and arranged for the family to move to the village. Villages were as far as a native doctor dared to go.

Nande was so young at the time of their big move. He missed what the family's benefactors had to say about life, death, and God.

The Carmos were never to return to the jungle. Many other families were to make the exodus to the cities from the jungles at that time. To most people starvation and survival instinct prodded them to make the move. The sociologists, in chronicling the trend, sanitized the ugly words. For them it was a problem to solve with some form of socio-political economics. Nande's five-member family seemed to follow the trend, but illness was the primary factor that took them first to the village and, later, to the big city. Nande was the last child and his mother was a sick woman after his arrival.

Survival in cities where dictatorship rules takes much more from people than they are equipped to give. But Nande's father had something he could sell. Using primitive tools, he had learned to build oxcarts. He adapted this skill to building simple houses for those who had the means to pay. He himself could not afford one. His earnings could

*never meet his family's survival needs. Home for them was
only the rented basements of less poor people. They had to
be moving from one basement to another. Not a difficult
undertaking, for there was not much to move in or out.*

*Mr. Carmo worked all day. His evenings were mostly
spent in the hospital where Mother fought for her life.
Neighbors watched the three children. The oldest was nine,
a girl who had been born prematurely and was always sick.
A brother came next. Nande was five. For many years,
Nande could not understand how his father survived that
difficult time. Years later he found out that his father had
taught himself to read by reading the Bible the missionaries
had given him. That could have been his source of strength,
for they all survived. And, eventually they were all under the
same roof. The Carmos became just another family trans-
planted from the jungle to the sprawling, naked suburbs of
the big city. In America, the suburbs house affluent people
in two-car garage homes among trees and manicured lawns.
In Nande's country, the suburbs were filled with the poor
who had to work night and day to barely eke out a living.*

*There was no middle-class. One was either very rich or
very poor. The rich lived in well-guarded villas beyond the
suburbs, or in the city. The poor lived in the city suburbs or
in the shantytowns. These groups did not mix, or intrude
upon one another.*

*The rich lived in palatial homes with flower gardens,
cars, and servants. Solid brick or stone walls protected the
houses. Many had shards of broken glass embedded in the
top with a mesh of sharp barbed wire caracoled all around
the hidden property, like American prison courtyards. But
there the walls were meant to keep people out, not in. Only
servants, recruited from among the poor, were allowed in the
compound. They were the privileged few who knew how the
mansions looked inside. Nande only found out how the upper
class lived through reading, and, later on, by observation*

when he had to work near them.

Nande's first intelligent impression of his outside world was expressed by the word squalor. *Houses in the suburbs were built helter-skelter, any way the self-builder knew how or could afford to build. The houses were already old and crowded with growing families before wires, stretching from pole to ugly, untrimmed pole, reached them. Most people could not afford that luxury anyway. Just a matter of economics, as Nande was to write later. For water, the men dug deep, round wells with picks and shovels borrowed from one another. There were no sewers. For all practical purposes, sewers were considered as fringe benefits, city things, rich people's things. Telephone for most people was still an abstract word.*

Beautiful things did not surround Nande's childhood. Round about him there were only ugly sights, dilapidated or makeshift structures, ravaged nature, make-do things. There was hardly any wooded area left, just scraps of vegetation here and there, uncared for, unkempt. Indeed a matter of economics. Beauty and environmental tranquility were not necessary things, not even as adjuncts to living. Flowers were for the dead, not for the living. Those things were thought to belong only inside the shard crowned fences of the rich.

Yet, there were people in the city even poorer than the Carmos. These places, looking and seeming as if in another world, were filled with desolation and unthinkable poverty. Their section was called the shantytown. Something dark and heavy kept the country, older than America, from keeping up with its own needs. The poorest of the poor constituted the underground strata of society. They seldom walked in the street. Their children never entered schools or their parents a store or church. Others were aware of them, but acted as though they did not exist. They patched up a hut or piled up a lean-to built with anything they could find in the

/

city dumps. The more fortunate had found o
pieces of scrapped building material that the
dwelling place.

Few understood how they lived without a well or a ...
room. Nobody went into those shanties. Not even the police.
"You'll never come out of those places alive!" was the usual
warning whenever the subject came up in conversation. The
prison population came mostly from the shantytowns. But
the criminal was only caught when necessity would force
him out of his world.

Those wretched human beings attached themselves to the
city as barnacles attach to ship hulls. They could not survive
in the suburbs. Here too, it was truly a matter of economics
that made them neighbors of the rich people, not of the poor
ones. But the upper class, hidden in their fortified homes,
simply ignored their presence in the world. This reaction was
fostered by the country's careless philosophy of living
expressed as, "If your problem hasn't got a solution, you
have no problem." The government could also ignore the
problem since there were no elections to worry about.
Sociologists alluded to the problem in passing with no solu-
tions offered and the Office of Tourism simply steered well-
heeled foreign vacationers away from the shanties.

Nande early wondered whether all countries were like
his country. He found himself looking more and more within
himself in his search for what was beautiful and meaningful
in life. Souls cannot live without beauty, their staple food.
Beauty-starved children need to find it somewhere in their
surroundings, where it is ready to give them the nutritional
gift of itself. When they don't find it, the soul's own instinct
brings the children's attention to their inner world where
abstract beauty lies dormant, like in the fairy tale, waiting
for the child's first, tender kiss to wake her up. But hungry,
angry, frustrated lips are more prone to pout than to kiss,
and then beauty cannot awaken within.

Even as a child Nande knew that he was one of millions of other children who were suffering the humanity-adulterating syndrome ignorantly diagnosed as a matter of economics. He sensed that there was more to it than economics, but could not diagnose it. Nande wondered how many children successfully found beauty within themselves. Children do not talk about those things to one another. They don't command the right words to use. And few adults have ears that can hear. Later in life, some of those children would be seeing their names in print somewhere. A very few names were to be found later under a piece of doleful poetry, if they had been educated somehow. Others might be found in an account of the latest revolution. Still others might be written up in a hastily written overnight crime report.

Nande himself barely escaped having his name on the annals of revolution when still a teenager. Later he was to meet a contemporary who grew up to become one of his country's leading criminals. This man saved Nande's life, and that of his loved one, simply because his desire for the magic of beauty had not yet died. His late-coming kiss was no longer innocent, but still tender.

Most children in Nande's country didn't go to school at all. Not enough schools were available. Understandingly, attendance was not compulsory. Elementary level was as far as a poor child could go, if at all. Those who went to secondary schools were fortunate. Schooling was an expensive commodity. Few families could afford it. The Carmos knew that their children's schooling would be finished when each reached twelve. Next step—work. Nande was twelve before he knew it.

What Nande wanted most in the world was to learn. Primary school and his zest for reading had opened wide for him a curtain into a complex world. How was he going to cope with turning his back to all that knowledge out there and learn to be content with his own introspective self? He suspected even then that a man is not an island. Man cannot live inside himself and still call it living. What Nande didn't know at twelve was that, even without schooling, he was about to enter the society of those who were to teach him to think.

CHAPTER 29

A Life Sketched

*H*is first employer was a dentist. He was a good man, with a quick smile and a big heart. He also had a pretty daughter Nande's age, Gretta. It was from her pretty lips that Nande heard his first dirty joke. He was first appalled, then confused, as she delivered the punch line and the giggle.

Dr. Salim didn't have an assistant. Nande was supposed to help him mostly by going after things and cleaning up. His office and lab were in his home so Nande was given home chores too. He hated every minute of his work there. They put him in a white coverall, the hem almost reaching the floor. Boys wore short pants at that time. Not familiar with the kind of apparel they dressed him with, he thought he looked like a girl. He was ashamed of his "gown" and tried to hide himself any way he could, especially from other boys.

He soon found out that simple exposure to the sights, sounds and life in the big city was a rich education in itself. Nande learned how the rich people lived. He saw his first kitchen with running water both hot and cold! He found public bathrooms. Most smelled bad, whether they were in restaurants or in public facilities. Years later, as he traveled *through many countries around the world, Nande learned to rate a country by how they cared for their bathrooms.*

The greatest of all discoveries he made that year was the public library. There had been no libraries in the schools he had attended. He could hardly believe his eyes when he saw for the first time all those books lining the long shelves. And he could read any one of them. For free! When told that he could even take one home he was ready to repent of all the bad things he thought about his country. He made the library his second home. There he spent his lunch hour and there he lingered whenever he had an excuse for not going home. That's when he had discovered the philosophers, and soon decided that the world of the mind was the one to which he wanted to belong.

Untutored, he was already trying to understand what Kierkegaard and Schopenhauer had to say in the books he found in the public library. They were followed by Lenin whose ideas Nande would soon find reason to bury. Freud was the rage then so he tackled him. Dictionaries were another of his happy discoveries. He always had one or two by him while reading.

It was a long walk to where the city transportation picked him up to take him downtown. It was a bumpy, jolting ride in streetcars the British had brought to the country. Nande wasted no time in these long rides; he read books with the whining of the electric motor and the ding-dongs of the conductor for background. He always traveled alone. He felt grown-upish.

There was a good explanation why Nande was reading heady writings at the tender age of twelve, especially the kind of philosophers who had so influenced our Western culture since the nineteenth century. One might think there is something wrong with a youngster spending time reading Nietzsche and actually enjoying what he is doing. But the boy had a desire to know answers to his many questions for

*which the thinking men of the past and present surely had
answers.*

*What disturbed Nande most, especially that first year of
his forced adulthood, was his feeling toward his country.
Through his readings, he had learned that love of country
comes early and naturally to growing children. But that
didn't happen to him. As a child, he actually felt uncomfortable with his country and countrymen. He practiced drawing the flag, trying to show the wind blowing it. He sang all
the patriotic songs. But he didn't have his heart in those
activities. He knew perfectly well why he lacked country-
love. Becoming citified confirmed all his suspicions about
his country. Initially he summarized his feeling by saying
that something was missing in his nation's soul. After
working and practically living in the city, rubbing shoulders with adults, and reading the newspapers, he was able
to list the things that were robbing him of his love of country. But even after the list was made he still thought that it
was not what was there, but what was not there that
disturbed his young heart. It was much later that he was to
find out what was not there.*

*Nande often thought of what the Bible seemed to say
about countries—that each nation has an angel assigned to
it. Could it be that the soul of a country is the soul of its
angel? If so, that should explain why some countries are
good and others are bad. Did not the Bible say that there
were good and bad angels? Nande concluded that the angels
of the country with the swastika and of his own country were
bad ones. There was in his country a pervasive apathy
toward things of the spirit, toward anything that was morally
good and innocent. He didn't see much abhorrence of either
dishonesty or the demeaning of others. He didn't see much
genuine praise or pursuit of what was good. Deception and
pretension were common experiences everywhere, and even
expected and approved. Mistrust was considered a proof of*

intelligence. Nande detected a hidden cult of dishonesty. It manifested itself in the awe people had for public figures and famous people known to be criminals, yet smart enough not to be caught.

Nande guessed then, and lived to find out he was right, that politicians maintained their power by capitalizing on that awe. Each succeeding dictator possessed the quintessence of that baffling ability. It was essential for playing the higher stake. One slip and another man with more expertise in the art would be pointing the army's guns in his direction. One mistake, and position and life would come to a bloody end.

Nothing but raw, brute power backed the reigning authority. The people had no voice in the government, no protection against the ill-use of that power gone awry. Power in Nande's country was like last century's ponderous cannons let loose on a warship's deck in a heavy sea. As for a balance of power, the concept was nonexistent in people's mind. Injustice was everywhere. It was just something to be endured, or exploited.

All this had produced a devil-may-care attitude on the part of the populace. Cynicism was in the very air the people breathed. The result was that there was an atmosphere of irresponsible laissez-faire everywhere. That developed aloofness in relationships and studied superficiality that would avoid deeper involvement that might expose truth. The country's renowned gaiety which flared out as easily as peacock's tail feathers, only covered ugly feet. The common atmosphere of debauchery was not frowned upon, but considered a viable source of humor. Most accepted marital infidelity as normal, as long as the culprit was a male. In day-to-day reality, that acceptance found its expressions in attitudes as much as in actions. Infidelity was credited with making a man more of a man, a myth both sexes seemed to believe in. Because depravity was admired, those who did not stoop to it felt they had to keep their purity hidden. The depravity might not have been as generalized as that but very few people cared to be perceived as not participating in it.

The phone rang, pulling Mark up from a deep reverie. Shaking his head, impatient at the interruption, he frowned into the receiver, regretting his decision to even answer its summons. In ten seconds, he replaced it. Another telemarketing call.

Questions tumbled over each other in his mind. Who was this Nande Carmo? Where had Grandfather met him? What country was he from? Where was he now? Was he still living?

Shaking his head in wonderment, Mark pictured the twelve-year-old boy from the jungles devouring books he himself had found difficult in college. Was that possible? Could an ignorant child of the jungle attain such things so early?

Mark sat back in an easy chair and pulled the manuscript to him. On he read more eager than ever to find the answers to his questions.

CHAPTER 30

A Bitter Disappointment

*A*s Nande left the old red brick school building, he considered himself the happiest thirteen-year-old boy in the country. He didn't even notice the sad state of the park where the large edifice had stood for years. Park and building were cramped on all sides by a city growing wider and claiming more room out of the once sylvan area.

While walking toward his streetcar stop, Nande went over the test he had just taken. The years of learning by heart his favorite poetry had helped to sharpen his memory. Yep! He couldn't remember a single question to which he didn't have the right answer. He was in! Two more weeks and he, Nande Carmo, would be starting high school. In the midst of his happiness, a hint of "too good to be true" nagged him. His nihilist philosophers echoed the doubting words, but his childish enthusiasm managed to drown them all.

The announcement of the test had been published in the city's papers. Nande had seen the same notice affixed to the board at the entrance of the building. It was done in legalese, to be sure, but it sounded so truthful, so democratic. Why should he doubt it? Its message was clear: there were openings in the new wing of the government high *school for children passing the rigid aptitude test. Nande knew about the existence of government schools supposedly created to teach the brightest children among the poor. He had never heard of a child from among his peers who had earned that right to enter the official school. Disbelief prevailed among poor folks. But apparently, the opportunities had always been there. Someone must have failed to communicate the good news to his neighborhood school.*

Nande had read the biographies of Abraham Lincoln, George Washington Carver, and the other American heroes of humble origin who had become great men in spite of poverty. Carver's story had been a challenge to him. He was Nande's hero. Maybe there was hope for his country yet. Nande should have known that they would not allow good minds to go to waste. Gratitude mingled with joy. And he knew he had earned it. There was no longer a doubt in his mind. And that was to be only the beginning. Next would be college, law, philosophy, literature. The world was opening its door to Nande Carmo.

He would have to find another job, as the classes were in the daytime. He knew of an early morning job delivering newspapers door to door in the city. Before going back to the dentist who had allowed him time off for the test, Nande stopped at the newspaper office. Yes, they would be glad for his services when the time came. Nande went back to work whistling the latest hit tune.

He was still whistling when he entered the government school building two weeks later. The announcement had stated that the names of the lucky children would be posted on the board on that day. Further information would then be given about uniforms, schedules, and the needed school material to be requested at the office. Nande expected the place to be crowded with children and anxious parents. But there was no one there except an old gentleman with white hair and kind eyes sitting at the information desk. He watched

Nande as the boy approached the rostrum on the board.

There was a long list of names of the future high school students. They were in alphabetic order. Nande's eyes went quickly from the A's to the C's and concentrated on that initial letter where he expected at any moment to read Carmo, Nande. His name was not among the C's. He brought his eyes to the N's. There could be a mistake in filing. He didn't find his name there either. Nande had stopped whistling. He felt his pulse increase. He went quickly through all the names on the five sheets of paper. His name wasn't on any of them. How could this be? By then he was unsuccessfully fighting tears.

The government employee was still watching him. Nande thought to hide his tears from the old man, but he was too late. The man had already left his seat and was walking toward him. He gently put his arm around Nande's shoulder. What he said then was to ring in the boy's ears for years to come: "You poor boy! You won't find your name there. This list was prepared before the test was given. It's all fake." Then, pointing to the five-page list he continued, "These are government employees' children—influential people—bribes—you know how things are—"

CHAPTER 31

Banners Pulled Down

*T*he Third of July Center was the largest Communist cell in the city and Nande was the latest 'member.' He had just turned fourteen. The year was 1936. The Second World War was soon to start decimating people in Europe. The worldwide Communist movement was getting into full gear. Nande had not decided yet whether to call himself a Trotskyite or a Leninist. Debates were hot in the cell in the evenings when the members got together in one of the barrios of the city after work. The place they met was halfway between downtown and the suburb. Here there were only brick houses next to one another, narrow streets, some paved with cobblestones, some still plain dirt. Children played in the streets. They had never seen or heard of a playground. The word never existed in their language.

The room was a large, converted car-garage that had somehow fallen into the Third of July's hands. You could still see grease spots on the cement floor and walls, leftover from its former use.

Nande was too young to have his name officially entered in the communist cell's books as a member. But the grown ups were impressed to hear the boy quoting Lenin and

Engel, and allowed him in. Besides, they soon found out that Nande was good at lettering signs. And there were plenty of posters to be prepared for the demonstrations and for the ever-sacred propaganda.

Had Nande actually become a communist? He could not answer that for sure. The anger he felt had to find an outlet. He despised his country for its deceit and prevention of his development into a wholesome, successful individual. His gentle sister had died that year in their latest basement home. She was just seventeen. Leukemia. The grim statistics had caught up with the Carmos with a vengeance. The only witness of his grief had been the tall walls surrounding his tiny basement backyard where he cried without anyone stopping him.

George Washington Carver and his America were very much in Nande's mind in those days. Would Carver have joined a cell like this in his search of success as a human being? But down deep, Nande knew that the question was only academic. Nande knew that Carver had overcome his social handicap not because his country had given him something, but because of what he and his nation were. What that really was he still didn't know. More than ever, he believed that there was something magic about America. Something that had to do with her soul. Nande was searching everywhere for what that was. He knew that when he found it, he would find himself too. At that time, he started thinking of America as a sister.

The Americans Nande met were either businessmen or missionaries in the city church his family went to. When the city missionaries spoke in the church Nande tried hard to guess through their presence and words what it was that America had that other countries did not. He never found that out through them. They talked much about being good and working toward improving the social condition of the people. But he was hearing the same thing with much fervor

and commitment from his books and, now, from his commu-
nist cell friends. Nande enjoyed the sessions at The Third of
July where the good of the people, the proletariat, was
placed, at least dialectically, at the top of their agenda. That
this good thing would possibly have to be accomplished
through violence was for him, at that time, a necessary and
logical postscript. But so grand an undertaking would never
come to that, he was sure. It would be like the promising of a
spanking never delivered because the child behaved.

Nande was grateful for what the jungle missionaries
had done for his family and for him. If it were not for them,
Nande would be still in the jungle, learning from his father
how to hunt wild pigs. He would have never learned to
read. He wouldn't have known that there was a wide world
out there filled with marvels and magic. He suspected that
those missionaries who had come to the jungle had the key
to unlock the secret of who America really was. What they
had to tell must have been important for they had risked
their lives to do it. The heart of their message seemed
somehow lost in tangles of words and meanings just as
Nande's would-be name had been lost in his father's mind.
It could not be the same thing he heard from the city
missionaries. Whatever the Stanleys told his parents years
before changed their lives and set them in a new direction
that led them to a more meaningful existence even in the
midst of poverty. He couldn't see how what he was hearing
could have done the same thing.

At fourteen, Nande was striving to see that his anger
didn't turn into hate, for he could see it advancing from afar.
He had found beauty and avidly nourished his soul with it.
The beauty he loved was in the colorfulness and power of
words and in the breath taking landscape they could paint.
He had also found beauty in the variety and depth of human
expressions and unselfish deeds. Nande knew that allowing
hate into his life would be suicidal to his soul. The cult of

beauty had become his religion. He looked at plastic arts, music, and literature as his religion's main denominations. His permanent membership was in the literary one.

Nande worried at this time whether he was betraying his 'sister' America by joining the Communists. He had concluded that the answer depended on whether he was right in thinking that whatever America had, came with her birth, and had not been acquired as she grew up. If that were the case, there was not much Nande could do. He would just continue to celebrate the good fortune of his 'sister' and seek to find the best for his sorry' mother', once his acquired nihilism and anger wore off. He still had hopes of loving his country someday. And that love of country would be needed, too, if what America had could be shared and practiced by other countries. When Nande thought of those things, he wished he had George Washington Carver there to help him find answers. Would he have known what the real message the Stanleys had carried to the jungle was?

The big demonstration was to take place at a large plaza downtown. There was a theater at the center, with businesses and offices encircling it. Not a single tree grew in the wide area between the theater and the surrounding businesses. You could see only cement and the cobble-stoned streets between the open area and the surrounding buildings. There was always a crowd of people milling about or walking through, especially in the evenings. The place was called Concord Plaza, or Place of Agreement. Nande liked that name.

On the day of the well-planned big demonstration, Nande's posters were ready. He was proud of his work. His job done, others had been assigned to carry the posters and to seek to draw the public's attention to them. Nande had been instructed to just stand by, watch, and learn how to go about coming out of the underground and into the public arena. That suited him fine, as his introspection and unassuming presence would never allow him to call the crowd's attention to himself. His new friends seemed to realize that too. But before the evening was over, he found out that they knew something else that he did not. And they were not ready to tell him.

The demonstration started quietly, his posters waving in the breeze atop poles held by strong hands. It was about seven in the evening. The weather was balmy and the crowd was huge. Nande sat on the steps of the theater and watched the march, all ears and eyes.

It was not long before he caught a growing murmur interspersed with catcalls coming out of the crowd. The words, so far, were not audible. But the volume increased. As time went by the shouts became more numerous and louder. Nande could distinctly hear what they shouted and he didn't like what he heard. There was not much agreement in that plaza. He heard his friends answering back, and that, too, was not aimed at producing concord. Nande was becoming fearful. What exactly was taking place here? How was it to end up? He found himself breathing hard. He saw one of his posters shake violently over the crowd before suddenly disappearing. More shouts and screams. People were running and dashing about. The Plaza of Concord was then filled with a confusion of sounds and movements. More of Nande's posters were destroyed after shaking uncontrollably in the air above the crowd. Violence was everywhere.

Then, without warning, mounted riot-police galloped into the plaza, coming from all four intersections as if on cue, their whips lashing out left and right. The loud screaming mingled with the clapity-clap of horses' metal shoes hitting the cobblestones. A gunshot echoed in the streets. More shots followed. Nande threw himself on his face on the cement. He was terrified and more lonely and despairing than ever before. But even in the midst of this dangerous predicament, he was able to think clearly. In a flash, he knew that violence was not to be only a postscript. The communist movement actively sought it; they would never be able to accomplish anything without it. Nande knew immediately that he had come to the end of the detour he had taken in his angry retaliation. He wanted out of that road. But what if the detour had led him to a dead end?

Nande jumped to his feet and ran. Dodging blood and bodies on his way out of that ill-named plaza he broke free and ran all the way home, miles from where the postscript had become a present reality for him.

Nobody was home when he got there. He took refuge in the small back yard behind the basement. He dropped down on the cold dirt and lay still, panting from fear and exertion. Mentally, Nande buried the ideas of Lenin and Trotsky in the soft backyard dirt beneath him. He would never find out whether he would be a Leninist or a Trotskyite. The gentle boy shuddered at the thought of all the violence he had witnessed that evening. He later learned that Trotsky died with a Mexican machete planted in the back of his head, and that Nande's compatriots who had died that evening were to be numbered among the millions Lenin's weapon of words had killed.

CHAPTER 32

Struggles for Education

❧

*T*he plantation was not large. It produced just enough fruits and vegetables to supplement the staple of students and staff. If any was left, it was sold in the local market.

Once again, American missionaries had come to the Carmo's rescue. One of the missionaries in the big city noticed the two Carmo boys' talents and secured for them a place in their mission-run school. It was a private high school just like the other secular schools, which were run for a profit. The Americans had built the school nearly five hundred miles away from the big city. Wealthy farmers and businessmen from various parts of the country sent their children there for their education. Students were accommodated in large dormitories. Nande never saw the inside of those accommodations. The plantation was a few miles away from the school buildings. There was a large shed in the center where the farm equipment necessary for the work was kept. Next to it, a naked redbrick addition served as a dormitory for the workers. Nande was one of them.

Years before, American missionaries had started the school when the world seemed more concerned with the hereafter than with earthly social struggles. It was located *halfway between Nande's big city and the little village where his father had registered him with the wrong name when he was born. The school was open to anyone, saint or sinner, who could afford to pay the tuition fees. There were no religious classes. A church in town catered to those interested in that subject. Nande ended his high school years there with nothing to show for spiritual enlightenment. But he never forgot hearing the school principal telling some teachers in the entrance hall "... I don't even let my children read the Bible!" Those words summarized for Nande all those years spent in a religious high school.*

He worked half the day in the field and went to classes at night. Nande was grateful to have the opportunity to pursue his studies. Yet, he was not happy there. He felt something was missing in the whole set up. Part of his dissatisfaction was that he never felt a member of the student body. He thought himself an outcast. Nande could not participate in the school activities, not even in the sports. Perhaps the administration felt that working in the fields was enough for a growing boy's physical exercise. There was in the school a class distinction no amount of religious talk could erase.

By then Nande was through with his former Marxist teachers. He was not going back to them to solve the problem of inequalities in human society. America had never needed to rely on Engel's socio-economic theories to become so great a nation. A country that was prospering not only economically, but also in societal and personal freedom must know something that the rest of the world did not know. Nande still suspected that the Stanleys, the missionaries that had helped his family escape the jungle, knew the secret. But why was that important message kept from the city people? Nande's parents hadn't seemed to know the right words to pass that secret on to him. The new wave of missionaries coming to the country were using some of the same words

Nande had learned from the secular dialectics of theorists like Engel and his school of thinkers. Now religious people were trying to fit secular society's pursuits into the single word Gospel. *Nande interpreted this mysterious word as being reshaped to accommodate those pursuits. Jesus was being portrayed as a social reformer, some kind of glorified Engel. Nande knew something was wrong with this teaching. But what teaching was right he didn't yet know.*

Even while Nande filled his mind with historical and scientific facts in classes, America was giving proofs to the world of her uniqueness as a nation in a war she never sought. The costly battles for human freedom she had fought before within her borders were being waged in foreign fields. Her costs in terms of her children's lives and her fortune were more than any other nation was paying. What was the secret of her strength and willingness to sacrifice so much to free the world from tyrants? How one nation could do all this was still a mystery to Nande. That was all part of 'the great American puzzle'. He was determined to put that puzzle together. This was at the top of Nande's agenda for his life, the main goal that motivated him to study hard, even after hours of work on the plantation during the day.

Nande figured that if he were ever to solve "the puzzle that is America" he would have to master English, the original language of the instruction book. He couldn't afford a dictionary; so he decided he would teach himself English the way children learned to speak and write. He would seek to learn new words and their sounds without bothering with their counterparts in his own language. That way the English words themselves would reveal to him their various shades of meanings as he read or heard them used in different settings. Nande spent hours reading books in English and trying to figure out what the strange words were saying. There was no such thing as tape recorders then, so it took a while to learn how the words were to sound. He had some difficulties with a few of English's hardworking words. He kept reading about all the different things that were made out of scratch. Hearing one of the missionary kids refer to a small wound in his arm as "just a scratch" would throw him off. But eventually he got the language figured out. By the time Nande started college in the capital, working all day this time and taking classes at night as before, he could read and speak English fluently.

It didn't take long for Nande to adapt himself to the sophistication of life in the capital of the country. His knowledge of English got him a good job in an international company. He lived in a student house connected with the private college where he took classes. Nande spent all his free time in the local public library. He tried to find American history books in English, written before the 20th century. He couldn't find any.

Nande soon discovered that the vocabulary and expressions of humanist historians was similar to that of the new missionaries. He had hoped that the words from the pulpits would throw some light on the birthing of America. It seemed to be a chapter of history modern historians wanted kept in the dark. It was not until a few years later that he was to find books in the New York public library with the very words of the Pilgrims and of the other writers of that period. He was later to master American early history when getting a degree in history from Columbia University. His "puzzle that is America" was to get shuffled badly when he had to read the revised history textbooks demanded at the university. It was a long time before he could rearrange the pieces back in the places he had already found for them.

During the years when he was struggling to get an education, both in high school and then in college, Nande's love for his country had not flourished. Democracy as an idea was often written and sung about in his country, but there was very little of it in the nation's politics. Sociologists and economists vainly attempted to explain the present socio-economic problems of the country and some offered solutions, but none of them materialized. Infant mortality was still painfully high. The majority of the people were still illiterate. People were still dying of hunger. There were plenty of academic dissertations on the causes for the country's ills. Most of the writers meant well, but the primary cause, the real reason behind the social and economic diseases of the country, was a matter of dissension among them. The disagreements, when reaching the political arena, often became violent. A few brave crusaders lost their lives when perceived to be a threat to the dictatorial power of the day.

By the time Nande finished college there was a break in the political scene. In between dictators a temporary, proforma opening to democracy was granted to the country's weary population. Nande suspected that the toning down of the dictatorial power was something demanded in Washington. The positive response was really a clever act to entice dollars into the country via American businesses and the generosity of the United States government. During that brief period, over a dozen political parties were applying for a piece of the governmental, political, and economical power, with more dollars in the till. That only showed how divided the country was. Corruption and self-seeking increased in proportion to the loosening of the dictatorial reins. It was becoming evident that with increased freedom came also increased evil. That assured Nande that something else besides freedom and democracy was needed. That was something that was missing in his country's soul, something capable of keeping good, like freedom, from becoming an occasion for evil. Without this missing element, democracy, as a system of government, would fail. Could it be religion? But the country already had more churches than were needed to cater to the number of people who cared for religion. In the socio-political arena, religious leaders kept *adding a point here and there, mostly feebly, or apologetically, on how to improve things, but that to no avail.*

Nande's religion was still the arts, beauty. Literature was still his god. He had once been tempted to adhere to some form of God-acknowledging system of formal religion. It happened midway through his college years in the capital. One Sunday afternoon found him seated by the sea in a public cafe with a book open before him. Two ladies were distributing some literature around to the patrons. Nande accepted the pamphlet given to him. It was a religious tract. He read the familiar Bible verses and commentary. It was written in up-to-date verbiage indicative of the political role being given then to religion. On the back of the tract, there was a poem. It looked familiar to him. After reading the first verse Nande remembered having written the sonnet himself at the age of fourteen, while a would-be member of a communist cell. His name was dutifully printed on the tract. The poem was about choosing to be good in an evil world, and explaining why you should be good. The writer of the tract had taken it from an anthology of religious poetry.

Nande was moved by the sounds of his own innocent words echoing his childhood's yearning for a yet unattainable goodness. Could the religionists be right? Was studied goodness the only attribute people and nations needed to succeed? Was this the clue he needed to put "the puzzle that is America" together? But then he remembered the well-meaning posters he had drawn at the same time he had written the sonnet. He saw again his banners shaking violently above the heads of the crowd in the Place of Concord before being dragged down. He heard the angry shouts and saw again the blood and the bodies on the sidewalks. He thought that all that came under the heading of good. No, there was something else besides goodness needed to change people's natures and nations' lives.

CHAPTER 33

The Boss

*G*eneral Koufi was in the inner circle of the latest dictator, and was the owner of the private college where
Nande was. The General needed an interpreter unexpect-
edly. The military politician was to entertain a high-ranking
official from the United States and his regular interpreter
was not available. That Friday evening Nande was in the
dean's office when the "Boss," as the general was known in
the school, had his call transferred to the dean's phone. The
caller had asked for Professor Isac, the English teacher of
the college.

"General," Nande heard the dean say, "Professor Isac
is a sick man. He checked in at the General Hospital this
week—" Nande watched the dean receive an earful and
understood by the dean's body language that General Koufi
was not happy. The "Boss" was a demanding officer and
hated to find himself in a situation where he had to depend
on others. Nande did not know it yet, but he was to have
many dealings with the General in the years to come.

"General Koufi, I think I have a solution for your
predicament. One of our students knows English as well as
Professor Isac. Isac told me that himself—" Again the dean

was interrupted for a few seconds before proceeding. "Yes, General, he happens to be here in my office. We—"

All the General needed to know was that there seemed to be a solution to his problem.

"I am sure Nande is available. Let me talk to him." Then, covering the phone with his hand, and turning to Nande, "Can you spend the weekend with the General Koufi and interpret for him?" Noticing Nande's wavering, he added, "He has a big bark, but he seldom bites."

"I guess I can," Nande answered timidly, "I have nothing planned this weekend that can't wait." The dean looked relieved. He took his hand off the mouthpiece.

"He's all yours, General. If he is as good as Professor Isac says your problem is solved. Would you like to talk to him yourself, Sir?" The General did. Nande was given the telephone and after a quick "Yes, Sir" all he heard was a long instruction. While filing in his mind the information he was receiving from the authoritative military man, Nande was glad he was not an aide-de-camp to General Koufi, the closest man to the country's dictator. Happily, he was being asked to serve the big man for only a couple of days. Nande never guessed then that his life would no longer be the same after that weekend. That telephone call marked the beginning of a new chapter in his life that was to influence the remaining chapters of his life. Nande was twenty-five.

General Koufi had lost his only son when General Zuki, the previous dictator, had successfully waged a coup d'etat on the dictator before him. The boy had been recruited to serve at the palace and one of General Zuki's bodyguards had shot him. The killer claimed that the young Koufi had reached for his pistol and was about to shoot his chief. But his father knew that the young soldier had been killed simply because he was the son of General Koufi, an officer of the army faction that opposed Zuki.

General Koufi was clearly impressed with Nande Carmo.

His interpreter behaved like a gentleman. He had followed instructions well. The General was able to communicate effectively with the official from the Washington's State Department. The "Boss" had no patience with disturbance of any sort and, thanks to Nande, there had been no incident to mar the weekend. By the time he had dismissed Nande late Sunday evening from the nightclub where the American was entertained, the General was treating Nande as a son.

Nande graduated a week later. The General had asked the Dean of Students to have Nande meet him at his office after the graduation exercises. The proprietor of the school rarely used that facility, but he made sure it was always available when he needed it. He had often entertained powerful political figures in the luxurious office with its leather couches, conference table, and liquor cabinet. Many important political decisions relating to the country and to the popular college had been made in that office. Now it was Nande's future that was about to be cast there.

When Nande came in, General Koufi was seated comfortably on the sofa, smoking a cigar. He got up to receive the student.

"Congratulations, Nande. The school is proud of you. Have a seat. How about a cigar?" He uncovered the wooden box of Cuban cigars sitting on the coffee table and extended it to Nande.

"Thank you, General; I appreciate your congratulations and your offer of a cigar. I take the first, but I am afraid I have to decline the second. I never took up smoking."

"How about a drink—oh! I remember now. You don't drink either. Well, good for you. Is that against your religion?" He asked in jest.

"No, Sir; just against my taste. I have nothing against it."

By this time, they were both seated on the same couch. Nande felt out of place, but at the same time, sure of himself. After all, he had just finished fulfilling one of his childhood dreams. The General looked thoughtfully at the young man before him. Nande waited for what Koufi had to say.

"Young man," he finally asked, after a series of puffs on his cigar, "What are your plans now? I want you to make good in life."

"Thank you, General. I appreciate your interest in me. I plan to go on to a good university. I want to study history."

"You always had to work, Nande?"

"Yes, Sir. Since I was twelve."

"You cannot study in a university in this country and work at the same time. You know that. Have you any means to meet your needs and pay tuition for the next four years?"

"No, General. I intend to work as long as I can for at least three years and save enough money to free myself from work for the next four."

The General looked amused. Before puffing at his cigar again, he revealed the reason for his humor. "Not with our kind of inflation, boy. Unless you are an extremely smart investor and lucky enough, the money you save in three years of work will probably buy you a couple of textbooks by the time you go back to school." Then, seriously, "That will not do, you know?"

Nande, the dreamer, had never thought seriously about this problem, though the General's contention had occurred to him. He had distanced himself well from his pessimistic philosophers. His new optimism was about to pay off.

"I have a better idea. How would you like to go to a university in America?"

Nande's mouth actually fell open. He could not believe his ears. Before he could doubt what he heard or dismiss it as a tasteless joke, General Koufi said, "Our Treasury Ministry keeps an office in New York City to handle all our international finances. We need an in-house translator there capable of handling both languages. If you are interested, I'll see to it that you get the job and work your own schedule.

That should free you to study. I understand that American universities are not like ours. Their system of credits makes class attendance flexible. Great country for students— America is!"

"Great country for many other things," The seriousness of the General's offer gradually became evident to him. For a second, the face and words of a white haired government employee, his hand on the shoulder of a thirteen-year-old Nande came to his mind. This time the vision just accentuated his joy.

"General Koufi, this is a dream come true for me. I am at loss to know what to say, except that I feel very grateful and will do my best not to disappoint you."

The boss looked pleased. Man of action that he was, he stood up. Nande stood with him. While shaking hands, the General added, commanding, not informing, "It is all settled then. You'll be paid well. In dollars. Be ready to leave in a couple of weeks. Call at the Ministry of Finances office on Monday and introduce yourself. I'll have someone there to take care of your papers. You'll need a diplomatic passport, airline ticket, and all that. They know what to do. Come to my house before you leave. We'll have a little good-bye party for you." Then, jokingly, "Dismissed!"

Nande walked out of that plush office seeing himself entering triumphantly through doors he never thought would be opened for him. In the midst of his happiness, he thought that now he would have to start fanning the fires of country-love in his heart. But his country was not to make the resolve easy for him. Just before he was to leave for New York City, Nande had to go to the other office General Koufi maintained at the Presidential Palace. For some reason his Pan-Am airline ticket was sent there. As he was crossing the well-guarded area outside of the building, he heard shots. He quickly realized that he was caught between two opposing and invisible weapons. Nande sprawled on the cement as he had done eleven years before. He spent one of his last hours in his country flat on a dirty floor while bullets were, again, flying over his head.

The attempted coup was foiled and, this time, no one was killed or hurt. At least that was what the public learned from the government-controlled media.

The farewell party at General Koufi's mansion took place as planned. Just the family, the wife and two daughters younger than their guest, were present. The General treated Nande as a son. So much unexpected attention made Nande wonder whether the "Boss" was aiming to eventually make him part of the family. Nande was not ready for that, and he wanted none of it. He was glad he would be out of the country within a few hours.

The Second World War had just ended, with America paying the lion's share of the cost in order to lead the free world to victory. Here was a nation ready to sacrifice the lives of thousands of her children on foreign soil, ready to spend millions of dollars—yet with no desire to dominate, although she had the power and even the right to do so. Germans would still speak German after the war. Italians would still speak Italian; France, French; and Japan, Japanese. This was a nation conquering to liberate others, not to expand or fulfill personal greed. Where did America's zeal for human freedom and dignity come from? These questions fueled his desire to figure out the nation's identity, so linked with his own.

Mark turned the page, expecting to find out what had happened to Nande in America, and whether he had achieved his goal of putting together 'the puzzle that is America.' Much to his dismay, the page he had just read seemed to be the final page of the manuscript. The pages that followed contained a profusion of notes and outlines still waiting to become the continuation of the narrative.

CHAPTER 34

Imprisoned!

❦

With a sigh of disappointment, Mark searched the notes further. Among them, he found another page completed, but it was not much. The narrative just begged for more tidings.

Nande's and his wife's prison was a sumptuous villa overlooking the ocean and miles away from the next dwelling or business. Beauty was everywhere. Outside the bay windows, a full moon mirrored itself on the limpid ocean waves billowing gently on their way to a whitish splash on the sandy shore. Inside the living room, the lights were off. It was from this darkened place that the two young men, sitting on comfortable couches, contemplated the lighted scene outside. Katie sat at the white grand piano by one of the windows. Nande's wife was running her trembling fingers over the ivory keys and bringing out of the hidden strings the gentle, magic sounds only she seemed able to produce. Her music betrayed her sadness; she was crying as she played.

Almost buried in the softness of a cream-colored sofa at the other end of the large window, Cory Boter looked handsome under the moonlight. Nande could see, as he did in previous evenings, that Cory was moved by the soft music played in that atmosphere of quietness and beauty. The moonlight glow bathing his face revealed that his eyes were brimming with tears. Cory Boter was Nande and Katie's jailer. This was the young couple's eighth day of captivity.

Nande felt the sting of tears in his eyes as well. His memory replayed the scene of his first meeting with Katie. She had played "Around the World, I Searched for You" in a school auditorium a world away in America. She had been accompanying him as he sang the romantic song for the school's international party on a Valentine's Day.

But how to explain Cory's tears? Nande had learned from the house servants that Boter had been raised in poverty before being plunged into crime and the luxury of his present living. Nande fancied that the beauty of the evening mingling with the magic of the sounds coming from the piano were leading Cory back to his destitute childhood, maybe to a spot where, in hate and anger, he had shrouded the sleeping beauty's face instead of kissing it. One thing was certain; Cory's soul was moved by the kind of beauty that leads to goodness.

While watching him unsuccessfully trying to hide his emotions, Nande thought of the changes he had gone through in the last four years. The events he sadly recalled spoke to him of the long, covertly moving tentacles of evil reaching out to him all the time, about to crush him. And the same fate awaited the one he loved the most.

After reading this brief account, Mark quietly sat with the manuscript in his hand for a long time. Apparently, Grandfather Targett had been too ill after writing those paragraphs to continue with the story. Mark knew then that he would have to plow through the many sketches and notations to find out more about Nande and his wife. Who was

Katie and how did they get to be house arrested and where? Had they been harmed? Had Katie escaped?

Three hours had gone by since Mark had started to read his Papa's manuscript. He put the reams of papers aside and absently opened the refrigerator. He was not hungry. His mind was full of Nande's story and its implications. Bypassing his mother's spaghetti he found lunchmeat in a plastic bag and made himself a sandwich. He munched mechanically, lost in thought. It would take much work, but Mark was determined to put together the rest of Nande's story at any cost. Mark decided he would study the notes and sketches with a view to keeping in order the sequence of the events they described. He would have to summarize them and try to finish the story without changing the style of writing he had detected in his grandfather's work.

Mark moved the papers to the basement where he had placed his computer the day before. It was cooler and more pleasant down there. He set up the computer on an empty desk and launched himself into the work.

CHAPTER 35

To Make a Long Story Short

Two days later, Mark had the events written down in chronological order. His summary of that absorbing life until the time when Nande and Katie found themselves in house arrest showed the sequence well. He added short notes to himself in parentheses to prod his memory when the actual writing began. Yet, even then, it seemed that Grandfather Targett did not have enough material there for Mark to plausibly finish the story. His notes, though numerous, left some holes. The story had no satisfactory ending. Mark set about studying carefully his outline to get the whole picture before attempting to continue the narrative.

His outline read:

- *Nande's first two-and-a-half years in New York were packed full of activity. (Describe.)*
- *He was determined to make use of the opportunity to fulfill his cherished personal dream of putting the "puzzle that is America" together. (Here include the 17th/18th century book he studied using the list papa made.)*
- *His lodging was in a second-rate apartment with kitchen privileges close to Columbia University. Nande*

gobbled up all the credits he could get in their history degree program.

- As an official translator for his government, he sched-uled his own time to work. (Describe here the trips to Philadelphia and Washington. Include his researches there.)

- Though grateful for the opportunity given to him, he still could not profess a love for his country.

- His work gave him a front seat in the criminal drama of corruption in which his own country's government engaged. (Include the annotated document Nande accessed to learn of the corruption.)

- The diplomatic personnel were at the heart of the coun-try's corruption. They abused their custom-free privileges by smuggling goods home to sell or to keep. (Use Papa's list.)

- Besides becoming rich with merchandising, they received exorbitant wages in dollars, some of their salaries higher than that of the American Presidents. (Nande had copies of salary checks among the other incriminating documents. Very important: that was the reason for his government later trying to incriminate him and confiscating all his belongings.)

- Diplomats were often called back home ostensibly for consultation, but in reality for perpetrating the smuggling activity.

- All this was happening while the poor people in the country were starving. (Papa had some statistics. Use them?)

- These disclosures made Nande feel as angry as when at fourteen he had joined the Communist Party.

- The knowledge that America had accomplished all that his communist cell mates wanted to accomplish in terms of social good and progress, yet without Communism, kept him seeking to solve "the puzzle that is America".

- Nande had a crisis of conscience for having become himself one of the privileged few. His first reaction was to quit his post and return home.

- He sensed a purpose for being in America. He could better solve the puzzle on location and later share it with his country.

- With that in mind, Nande started to document all the corruption he found. He hoped a venue would eventually open for him to use the information toward the eventual healing of his country. He wrote articles to accompany the papers he copied. Underground publications printed them.

- Nande lost his position three years after getting it. The latest coup was successful this time. General Koufi was out of power; Nande found himself out of a job. (Papa has a New York Times clip on this. Use it?)

- His country's government-controlled media reported that the former dictator had shot himself, but in truth, he was assassinated.

- Nande had by then enough money saved to be a full-time student. With his diplomatic visa useless, he had to secure a student visa. (There's a good report on Nande's first time experience of acquiring needed documents without having to bribe the government employee.)

- After getting his degree, he accepted a teaching job in a small town in New Jersey. There he experienced something of life in rural America, an enlightening and needed experience. There he met Katie, and there he met Mark Targett. (Fictionalize this part. Name the college and town?)

- Nande found Katie to be the loveliest person he ever met. She was talented, simple, and others-minded. She was pretty too.

- Katie taught music at the same college where Nande taught history. At an international valentine party for students and teachers, Nande was talked into singing. Katie accompanied him at the piano. They fell in love and got married in the little town where Katie was raised. (Too juicy a chapter not to elaborate.)

- Nande was approached by a journalist from his

country's top newspaper who knew all about Nande and his crusading to convert his country. He claimed there was a secret movement to democratize the country under America's tutelage. The newspaper wanted Nande to join them. Nande believed Cory's story and after much prayer, he and Katie accepted the airline tickets they provided for them to fly to Nande's country.

- Nande felt sure this political venture was to be his life's purpose.

- A week before leaving America Nande found out he was entrapped. Nande had accompanied his "journalist" friend and was waiting for his return from a plush store in Manhattan in what he thought was Cory's car, a brand-new, expensive vehicle. Cory had forgotten to lock the glove compartment. In it, Nande found a gun, papers from an automobile dealer in Delaware, and numerous one-thousand dollar bills. The vehicle papers showed Nande as the owner of the automobile. He discovered that Cory was his country's top smuggler and was connected with the government. He had a liaison also with the American underworld. (This should be well detailed.)

- Nande knew that his life was in danger. There was nowhere to run without risking hurting Katie. He figured they wanted only him. He felt that if he followed his government's plan without letting them know what he had discovered, Katie's life could still be spared.

- To make sure Katie, as an American, was not to have her life ruined, Nande described his situation in writing. After signing and sealing it, he left the document in the hands of his friend, Mark Targett. Knowing that others in the same circumstances had been killed, he and Katie left New York for what Nande thought would be his doom.

- As soon as the plane carrying them had landed in Nande's country, the two of them were escorted to a waiting car. They never went through immigration or customs; they

never saw their luggage again, including their carry-ons. As the car sped away toward their place of confinement, Katie, confused and scared, cried and asked questions Nande could not answer.

- Note: Papa never mentions the name of Nande's country, though he knew it and jotted it down. Decide whether to carry out that decision.

CHAPTER 36

A Thrilling Escape

Mark's summary of Nande and Katie's story just covered the gap between Nande leaving his country to go to America and his imprisonment. Mark's only hope of finishing the story was finding further material in his grandfather's vast correspondence. Accordingly, the next day he started delving into the letter file from the chest in the attic.

The more letters from his grandfather's correspondents Mark read, the closer he felt to his Papa. It was a most gratifying experience to see confirmed through the eyes of his grandfather's friends the same sentiments Mark had precociously entertained as a child. Papa's generosity, his honesty, his enduring faith, his warm humanity—all came across with pleasant clarity through those letters. His earnest Christianity became evident by the witness of others. Mark was so delighted with the experience that he momentarily forgot his main purpose for reading those letters. Then, halfway through the letter file, he found himself back again on the path of Nande's story. For some illusive reason, a couple of neatly folded pages had been filed with the letters. Mark was delighted to find that they belonged to the manuscript. The pages were either a continuation of the chapter Mark had thought was the last one finished by his grandfather, or they made up a new one. With those pages the narrative continued, apparently with no lapse:

The moon had left for the evening when Nande and Katie found themselves alone. But during the next day, Nande found out that the magic of the evening had worked in Cory's soul. Sometime during the night, it might have awakened the sleeping beauty still within him.

By mid-morning, one of the servants came into the Carmo's quarters to tell them that Cory Boter wanted Nande to see him in his office in a wing of the villa. Nande kissed Katie and went to see his jailer, his heart in his mouth. Cory was waiting. He was wearing a faint, guilty smile and, was again as friendly as when Nande had first met him in New York City. He bid Nande to sit down before his desk, then said, calmly, "Nande, I want you and Katie to get out of this mess." While speaking he opened the top drawer of his mahogany desk, took out a brown envelope, and handed it to Nande. Inside Nande found two passports, his and Katie's. He hadn't seen them since leaving New York. There were also two one-way tickets to Idlewild Airport in New York City and two crisp one hundred dollar bills. Those three items were self-explanatory. Before Nande could recover from his surprise, Cory was handing him a set of car keys. He sounded earnest and yet furtive when instructing Nande on what to do.

"Just before it gets dark," he directed, "go to my private parking lot in front of my garage. You'll find a DKW there already gassed up. My guards won't stop you. Drive off with your wife to the main highway, go past the town, and head for the capital. You'll find instructions in the car on where to leave it when you get there. You are to destroy the sheet of paper as soon as you memorize what is written on it.

Whatever happens, don't talk to anyone. And don't play any trick or you'll miss your only chance of getting away. I am taking a great risk to do this. Don't make a reservation to take the plane to New York. Hide yourself somewhere and go to the airport just before departure time. The airplanes are not full this time of the year. Make them believe they blotched your reservation. That's all I can tell and do for you. You can go, now. Good luck."

A cloudy sunset met Nande and Katie outside when they crept out to the garage. There would be no moonlight that night. It was as if the full moon the previous evening had only been a theatrical prop. It had fulfilled its purpose in the heart of a gangster and the stage master had it removed from the scene.

They located the car, slid into their seats, and were getting settled when they saw the loaded gun. It lay on the piece of paper with the instruction on what to do with the car in the capital. This was the first time Nande had held a gun in his hands. He had been excused from the army of the ruling dictator when he was eighteen for having lost fifty-percent vision in one eye. Would there be a need to use the deadly weapon? They each shuddered.

Nande turned the key and pressed the accelerator. The little, noisy Danish car responded quickly, with a roar. Not fully believing their release, they reached the highway in apprehension and prayer. As Boter promised, there were no armed guards anywhere. If they managed to board a plane to New York, they would have to start life anew. And six months from then there would be a baby for them to care for if their harrowing experience didn't affect it.

Nande no longer had his U.S. Department of Immigration card. At the embassy, they were told that it would take at least a month for it to be replaced. They couldn't travel until then. The visa officer interviewing them left them alone in the office with instructions to wait. The few minutes seemed like hours.

When he returned he was smiling. He told them he had a daughter back home about to become a mother too. He had found a way to waive the requirement. Nande and Katie were never told how the American officer managed it.

Two days later the Carmos were home. All they had left of their worldly goods were the clothes they wore when landing at the airport. Strangely enough, neither the airline nor the customs inspectors in New York enquired of them the reason why they did not have any luggage.

CHAPTER 37

The Letter From India

❧

It was very late in the third day of Mark's research by the time Mark finished putting together the body of his Grandfather's work. But he knew that the biographical novel was still incomplete as it was. The ending chapter could not be the end of the work. Nande as yet had never put together "the puzzle that is America." Despite the Carmos having escaped the intrigue with their lives, there was a tone of defeat in the story. That was not like his Papa and the book would not quite justify the title. There ought to be more to the story. Again, he turned to the letter file at the place where he found the last chapter of the manuscript. It was not long before Mark came across a long letter signed by Nande Carmo. But it was written from Bombay, India, in April 1970. Mark devoured it.

After the *"Dear Mark,"* the letter read:

"Your letter took a month to get to me. It bounced around Europe before being forwarded to India and I got it just now as we are about to pull out of Bombay harbor. I didn't want you to wait too long to get a reply, so I had better answer right away. I write in haste; so brace yourself for my long-sentenced writing you were always teasing me

about. I can't afford the time now to chop a sentence up for an easier understanding. And you'll have to put up with the barbarisms that sneak up on me when I write fast in a language that is not my own.

"It's so good to know your illness seems to be in remission and that you feel you'll be able to pick up on <u>America! America!</u> where you left it so long ago. I have been praying long and hard for you since I last saw you in New Jersey and you were drilling me for material for our book. You were even then a sick friend and it hurt me to see what was happening to you. But who are we to contest God? I left the U.S. with the assurance that if we were not to see each other on earth we would be continuing our conversation in heaven some day, our earthly concerns all gone then. One of the greatest joys of my life was seeing you become a Christian.

"I don't think I ever thanked you enough for taking my side in the college dispute about American history. I knew that eventually I would have to either adopt the revised text-books or quit teaching. As you know, I opted for the latter. You asked me for details about this decision. The answer will be forthcoming.

"About 'the puzzle that is America', the phrase which identified the center of my life and pursuits, I finally succeeded in putting it together when returning to America after my failed crusading sortie to 'save' my own country. I thought I had the puzzle close to a solution then, but I found out later that the two pieces still missing were extremely critical. I thought I could get away with sharing with my country what I had found that far. I learned that one cannot tuck a nation under God as a nurse tucks in a patient. It was only after I foolishly placed my dear Katie's life in danger that I found the missing pieces. When this happened, contrary to my youthful expectation, I realized that what America has can only come by birth or by rebirth. Life cannot be shared. Only what brings life can. You were too ill

when I last saw you for us to talk together about this. We both thought that you would not be able to finish the book. And I knew I had to do what I am doing now: sail the world in a gospel ship, this decision being a direct consequence of having finally solved the whole puzzle. But I am ahead of myself here. Let me start from the beginning.

"Here's 'the puzzle that is America' put together. You'll probably find me dictative, preachy now, but I see no other way of saying what I have to say. I think I can better accomplish this by using a series of phrases that delineate each piece of the puzzle. I'm doing it this way because I might have to stop writing before I say all that's in my mind. I intend to place this letter in the hands of someone ashore before the ship pulls out. By making a quick summation here, I will have shared with you all I found out about America's secret, though without further comments. That we'll leave for another letter. So, here's a simple analysis of America's DNA as I finally see it:

> *An 'in-the-beginning-God' of creation and absolutes. This Creator God creating humanity 'in His own image'. This divine image giving humanity its high value and dignity. As the Creator is eternal, so is His human creation. As the Creator can choose, so can His creation choose (free will in theology; there can be no true love without a choice). Free will as the fountainhead of freedom. Freedom unleashing good or evil because of choice. The more the freedom, the more the resultant good or evil. Good producing meaningfulness and life, evil producing meaninglessness and death. Redemptive work of an Incarnate God and historical Jesus, lessening now, and forever someday, the consequences*

*of evil to the ones so willing. The actual exis-
tence of an eternal nation to be gained when a
temporary one, even if made great for being
under God, ceases with time.*

"As a historian I have dug deep into the thoughts of the
Pilgrims (the First Comers, as the Quakers called them).
And as a late-coming Pilgrim, I analyzed their statements,
their political documents, their sermons, and their lives. I
came to three basic conclusions about America and her
founders: a) the founders that mattered most believed all
those things encapsulated above; b) they were in that state
of redemption as per the gospel they lived by, and c) they
were the ones who laid the rocky foundation of America on
those tenets. Our very Constitution reflects what I wrote so
far. The strength and greatness of our nation depend on the
integrity of those rocks, her decadence and death can occur
when one or more stones are removed or chipped away. The
knocking at her foundation has been going on since
America's birth. Freedom allows for that. No chipping or
stealing of stones succeeded until religious and secular
humanists mounted a concerted attack, still in progress, on
America's foundation.*

"Freedom is a risky thing. It allows you to even knock
out from under yourself the basis for the freedom to do it. To
use your freedom to do that is irrational. Secular humanism
is pure irrationality. To pursue it is to purposely extinguish
the soul of America.*

"Those tenets express the true meaning of the gospel as
those who conceived America learned from the Judeo-
Christian Scriptures. The word is to be found spelled out or
implied in countless historical documents. Such is the case
of "The Fundamental Orders," truly the birth certificate of
America. Even while defining the soul of the new nation,
this document also laid, for the first time, the foundation of*

democracy, something the Greeks were only able to talk about. Only a small minority of Americans ever heard of that historical document. Since humanism-led history revisionists have kept this and other historical papers hidden to the eyes of two generations of students, it is worth quoting here. I have it hanging here on my cabin wall:

> *"For as much as it hath pleased the Almighty God by the wise disposition of His divine providence so to order and dispose of things that we, the inhabitants and residents of Windsor, Hartford, and Whethersfield are now... dwelling... and well knowing where a people are gathered together the Word of God requires that to maintain the peace and union of such a people there should be an orderly and decent Government established according to God, to order and dispose of the affairs of the people at all seasons as occasion shall require: do therefore associate and conjoin ourselves and our Successors and such as shall be adjoined to us at any time hereafter, enter into Combination and Confederation together, to maintain and preserve the liberty and purity of the GOSPEL of our Lord Jesus which we now profess, as also, the discipline of the Churches, which according to the truth of the said GOSPEL, now practiced among us; as also in our civic affairs to be guided and governed according to such Laws, Rules, Orders, and Decrees...."*

"You probably will not need further elaboration on the sketch I just wrote on how I see 'the puzzle that is America' put together. Notwithstanding this, I plan to do that at sea, when I shall have more time. But how America's neglecting

of the verities of the gospel affected my life personally should be important for our book. By the time the jungle-born boy's eyes, ears, and mind were opened to the thinking of the forties, humanism had done enough damage to the foundation of truth and of America. For this reason, the boy could not understand the meanings of the gospel, God, or redemption under the definitions and practical outcome of relativism and higher criticism. And America herself, still basking in glory, thus became to him the puzzle that to put together had almost cost him his life.

"When back in America the wizened historian noticed how the chipping at America's foundation and the stealing of her fundamental rocks were already threatening the nation's collapse. Political conservatism alone could no longer preserve her 'American-ness'. What can a little one like me, plucked out of the jungle, do when noticing the hole in the western civilization dike? My answer was the same as that of the Dutch boy—plug the hole with his little finger and wait for help to come. That explains my joining the crew of this ship. Its sole purpose is to spread the Pilgrim's gospel that made America great. The gospel is the only thing that can keep America, Western civilization, and the world safe. I shall not abandon ship as long as the movement that launched it does not go astray from its purpose.

"I was just told that our pilot won't be coming on board right away. I should have more time now to write. So here we go.

With the puzzle now put together, here's the picture I see: The phenomenon of America is the unique result of an optimum God-humanity relationship. It is the spiritual finding its way into socio-economic human experience in a body polity. It is the historical, cosmic event of Creation's redemption giving birth to the degree and kind of human value and freedom that unleashes greatness. No political philosophy, history, or natural resource alone, can ever duplicate this phenomenon apart from a faith in the gospel of the God of absolutes.

"I am fully aware of how controversial my interpretation of America can be. For those to whom political philosophy, academically and subjectively understood, is the only source of reality worth considering, my interpretation is naïve—simplistic. Secular humanists might call it divisive, parochial, or 'better-than-thouness' at best. But I feel that unless God intervenes, the future history of America will be the history of the clash between two different ultimate purposes for humanity. The first is that of God's gospel-prepared, eternal, perfect kingdom with provisos of the Ten Commandments until then maintaining law and order for our temporary earthly life. The second is that of the secular humanists' earthly paradise, with an international judicial system adjucating under evolutionary laws. The first is the theme of the scriptures, which are being now rejected. The second is clearly spelled out in the Humanist Manifestos whose philosophy is being widely embraced. As America is taught to accept naturalism an individual's worth will no longer be valued by our Creator's currency (His own image), but by the cambists of hedonism. That will greatly facilitate the governmental transition to pure secularism, which always costs human lives. America's power and influence, once used for the liberation of individuals and nations, will be conditioned some day to champion the new form of oligarchic government implementing socialism. To accomplish this, sophisticated, democratic America, will not need the raw power of the gun. By voting God out of her political life, her courts will be free to usurp the authority of her two other powers to fit the new America for her "more enlightened" role in the new world. This is what happened in Nazi Germany. It could happen to America shortly.

"My coming to India, which for me is the embodiment of the East, sealed my interpretation of America in my mind

more than any other experience or conclusion. Any thinking individual coming to India will find his philosophy of life tested to the core, whatever that philosophy is. More so if, as a deist, you seek to understand God and His ways with humankind. Whatever your concept of God and of humans you'll be frustrated trying to interpret all you see, hear, and learn here in terms of social economy or in terms of a caring God. The first thing that will discomfit you here is the overwhelming numbers. Nearly a billion people, thousands of gods and goddesses, hundreds of different languages, thriving germs of all sorts, cattle, insects proliferating themselves without restriction, rodents voraciously consuming the scarce food supply of the land. My own first thought as I bumped into people walking, eating, chanting, ambling about, begging or lying down or dying in the sidewalks, I must confess, was a blasphemous one. The picture that came to my mind and which I had difficulty in evading was of God, like me, being addicted to peanuts. His appetite was enormous and, being God, the shells being thrown on the dirt would immediately sprout and grow into new human beings already hungering, thirsting, starving, suffering. Where is the high human value as appraised by God in the Scriptures? Eleven, I am told, is the number of people necessary to be legally certified as killed by a runway elephant before the animal can be put to death.

"If political socio-economics is not the answer, which it is not, here you have to conclude that religion is not the solution either, for India is an extremely religious country. Their many gurus are actively seeking to fill the spiritual vacuum being formed in the Western world, especially in America, with their asceticism devoid of redemption. Muslims are gearing up to accelerate their missionary work in America, encouraged by our innate religious freedom, oil, the high international value of the dollar, and the generosity of Americans. You can expect meditation carpets

and minarets all over the world before long.

"The eastern world's intense but sterile religiosity side by side with stark misery confirmed in my mind the two pieces I used to finalize the solution of 'the puzzle that is America': the sin-redemptive life and death of Christ and the redeemed's coming perfect kingdom. If there is no eternal afterlife, with all evil totally obliterated under a righteous government, our earthly, time-limited life is the cruelest of jokes—a joke that secular humanism will not tell because nobody laughs.

"Those two concepts found in the genesis of America—redemption and God's coming kingdom—give us the best explanation I know for America's affluence and the world's privation. The divine rule of abundance is the Judeo-Christian principle experienced empirically and historically by the Western World, which is, 'Seek ye first the kingdom of God and His righteousness, and all these things shall be added unto you.' The founders of America led the world in this path with gusto to become the greatest nation in human history. The two religious beliefs, one redemptive and the other redemptionless, one offering an earth-like, sensual paradise and the other righteous completeness are on a final collision course. It is just a matter of time before East and West find themselves in a deadly confrontation. Deadly for the soul because the battle will involve minds and hearts; deadly for the body because the combatants will be armed with weapons of mass destruction. Political philosophers then will only be able to watch the conflagration and fruitlessly voice their leftist or rightist credo before coming themselves to the finality of a world still waiting for a final redemption which is being refused. Our western world will realize then, too late, how that the spiritual is what determines the outcome of men's relationship to earth and to other men. The gospel of the Pilgrims is desperately needed today. That's why I keep my little finger in the hole I found

in the dike. That's why my small family and I sail from port to port in this gospel ship, which right now, incidentally, is ready to leave Bombay for Singapore.

"My time is up, Mark. I see through my porthole that the pilot is already climbing onboard. I will hand this letter over to a waiting ship chandler to post here in Bombay. This will save us a couple of week's time. I'll be writing again when not pressed by time. Do keep me informed about your health. I guess I told you before that I like the name you gave me in your book, our book, so much so that that's how I'll be signing my letters to you from now on. 'Katie' is well and sends you her love. Our little daughter is having a ball, sailing the world. Our school onboard is doing a good job in teaching our children. Needless to say, all of them are good in geography, and best of all, in the things of God. Must close now. God bless.

> *Affectionately.*
> *'Nande Carmo'"*

Mark finished reading the letter late at night, sat back, and evaluated what he had just learned. He realized acutely that there was more to his quest than just finishing a book. Nande's thoughts and life presented Mark with the greatest test yet to his mind about America and about his own life. Mark detected sincerity and intellectual honesty in the writer of the letter. Could Nande be right about America's identity? If he was, Mark's life and work were surely heading in the wrong direction, just as Abby said. But, then, was the writer for real? Could he be just a character Papa created in order to express his own beliefs? It seemed that his grandfather became a Christian around that time. Christians like Abby and her grandfather hold views similar to those of Nande. But someone else signed the letter as Nande Carmo. That could only be the individual whose biography Papa was writing—unless that was Papa's invention as well. The letter from Bombay was typed, the same as Papa's manuscript. No clue there. Could his grandfather have written the letter himself? And if so, why should he do it? Mark had his own puzzle to solve.

Mark reminded himself that Nande, if there was a real Nande, had come from a primitive jungle life; yet in a few years, he was teaching a college course. His mind was sharp and well developed, with no signs of being in the throes of nature's evolutionary convolutions. But, again, was there, or had there been, a Nande Carmo? Truth. Had Mark been conditioned to base his thinking in chameleon-like truths, as Abby had contended? Why had it become so important to him to find truths, truths that existed independently of his perception and angles of vision? Why did all the events of his life lately conspire to discredit everything he had learned so far? And then there was the Bible thing. *"In the beginning was the Word."* Word becoming flesh. Word and substance becoming one in a man. Creation through words, not a bang. Truth. Who is to have the final word? Who is to declare truth to be the Truth?

Mark was fully aware that he was in the midst of an intellectual crisis. Suddenly he felt tired. He pulled his chair back, got up, and climbed the stairs. He dropped into his bed and wished for sleep to come. But sleep shunned him. His brand new Bible was still sitting on his night stand. Mark looked at the leather bound book and remembered some of what he read the night before. "The words I speak to you, they are life." Where was it he read those words? He picked up the Bible, pulled himself up in bed, and opened the book at random. His eyes fell on a verse he had read before, but for a second, it seemed to be the only one on the page—*"I am the Way, the Truth and the Life...,"* it read. Who could make such claims? A quick glance at the preceding verses answered that question—Jesus.

A thought that never occurred to him before entered his mind then: "This Jesus is either hallucinating or he is, indeed, the Truth."

"The historical Jesus, the Christ, is the architect of our Western culture," Mark remembered reading somewhere. He knew enough history to know the truth of the statement. How could Jesus set the basis for culture while mentally unbalanced?

His tiredness was gone as quickly as it had assailed him before. A subconscious decision led him back to the basement and to his grandfather's papers. He sat again at the desk and again opened the letter folder. To his surprise, behind Nande's letter from Bombay, he found part of a yellowish envelope he had ignored before. It had been attached to the back of the last page as if glued to it. Mark loosened it and turned it over to see its front. The stamps were there. They were from India and had been cancelled in Bombay. The sender's name, though faded, was clear. Mark read the name and suddenly found himself face to face with Abby's Hound of Heaven. The sender of the letter from Bombay was Marco Nemo.

Suddenly, things became clear in Mark's mind. He had been deceived. He had willingly accepted the lies and acted upon them. Now, he would open his heart to the truth, as spoken in God's Word. Mark never felt trapped as the gift of intelligent faith was poured on Him by a gracious God.

CHAPTER 38

A New Beginning

When Helen woke up during the night and saw light coming from Mark's room, it was almost two o'clock in the morning. Again, she tiptoed to the door and looked inside. Mark was kneeling by his bed. Wisely, Helen retraced her steps in silence.

The next morning was a Sunday. Helen was already dressed when she heard noise in Mark's bedroom. Her son was awake and about. She came to the door and called, "Mark, dear, I'll be going to church in a few minutes. Breakfast—"

"Mother, wait for me. I am coming to church with you." The words were like music to her ears—sacred music.

As the two were entering the house after returning from church Mark made a solemn announcement, "Mother, I have something to do for Papa before I can go anywhere with my life. I owe him that much. We all owe him that much. I need to finish Grandpa's book. If it is OK with you, I am going to spend all my time here working on the manuscript. And, Mother, please do your son a favor. Go see Abby and tell her all about it. Tell her that the fox stopped running and found out that all the hound wanted was to lick the fox's wounds." Then, smiling at his mother's puzzled look, "That's OK, Mom. Abby will understand."

A few weeks later after the Sunday morning church service Mark started his car in the church's parking lot and headed for Canaan. A few minutes later, he veered off route 196 into Church Street. He parked his car across from Number 103 and waited. This time he didn't mind being seen. His heart palpitated, but gladly. In a few minutes, the old, red Dodge Caravan came up the curve with an elderly couple in the front seat. They waved to Mark before turning into the old farmhouse driveway. Mark waved back. The driver stopped the car, got out, walked around the Caravan, opened the passenger door, and helped his lady out of her seat. They looked again at Mark still in his car and again waved. Mark climbed out, stowed his brown leather bound Bible under one arm and picked up a thick folder. He might not need the Bible, but the symbolism was important to him today. The elderly couple waited for Mark to reach them.

"Good afternoon!" he said when facing the couple. "Can I visit with you for a few minutes, Mr. Nemo?"

"Certainly, young man. Let's go right in. It should be cooler inside." Marco unlocked the front door and held it open for Katie and Mark to come in. Closing the door behind him Mr. Nemo indicated a seat to Mark, "Please, have a seat while we finish arriving." He bowed in a pleasing, gracious manner. Mrs. Nemo smiled at Mark, "Old folks can't change pace too quickly, you know." They left the front room and disappeared behind a door. Five minutes later, they were back. They both sat across from Mark at a little table set beside the window.

"What can I do for you, young man? I see you are just returning from church too. You are..."

"I am sorry, Mr. Nemo. I should have introduced myself first. My name is Mark. Mark Targett." He got up and shook Marco's hand. They shook feelingly, and the old man didn't release Mark's hand. He seemed to have forgotten it was there. For a long time he looked into the young man's eyes, years of memories piling over one another under his snow-white hair.

Finally, he cried, "Mark Targett! Would you be my old friend, Professor Mark Targett's—"

"—Grandson," Mark finished. "Papa willed his manuscript of your life to me, Mr. Nemo. It was first placed into my hands a few weeks ago, upon my graduation as a journalist. It seems that without my knowing it, my whole life and experience have been conditioning me to answer his prayers for the completion of your story. I'm ready if you are."

The couple exchanged glances long and pregnant with meaning. "I am ready and honored," Marco answered. "There is a fifty-year gap to be filled, Mark. We will have to visit for a little longer than your few minutes." Marco Nemo's eyes twinkled roguishly.

"As long as it takes, Mr. Nemo," Mark replied determinedly. I have Papa's work finished as far as 1951, when you and Mrs. Nemo returned to America. I'm looking forward to working with you until this story is fully told.

Mark, his hand released, handed the manuscript over to his new friend. Marco opened the folder and read:

Mark Targett got ready to work through another uneventful day. He hated sameness as much as he hated his temporary job. Tuesday was usually a slow day at the electronic store. Quitting time seemed like an eternity away. Then suddenly, by mid-morning, things changed abruptly. The sameness that bored him so would not return...

Printed in the United States
41005LVS00003BC/118-513